WARNING

This book contains sexually explicit scenes and adult language. It may be considered offensive to some readers. This book is for sale to adults ONLY.

* * * * * * * * * * * * * * * * * * *

Please store your files wisely where they cannot be accessed by underage readers.

Copyright 2015 by Revelry Publishing

All Rights reserved under International and Pan-American Copyright Conventions. By payment of required fees, you have been granted the non-exclusive, non-transferable right to access and read the text of this book. No part of this text may be reproduced, transmitted, downloaded, decompiled, reverse-engineered or stored in or introduced into any information storage and retrieval system, in any form or by any means, whether electronic or mechanical, now known, hereinafter invented, without express written permission of the publisher.

DISCLAIMER

This book is a work of FICTION. It is not to be confused with reality. Neither the author nor the publisher or its associates assume any responsibility for any loss, injury, death or legal consequences resulting from acting on the contents in this book. The characters, incidents and dialogue are drawn from the author's imagination and are not to be construed as real. While reference might be made to actual historical events or existing locations, the names, characters, places and incidents are either products of the author's imagination or are used fictitiously, and any resemblance to actual persons living or dead, business establishments, events or locales is entirely coincidental. Every character in this book is over 18 years of age. The author's opinions are not to be construed as the opinions of the publisher. The material in this book is for entertainment purposes ONLY. Enjoy.

ISBN-13: 978-1988083346
ISBN-10: 1988083346

Other Books by Carla Coxwell:

<u>Fifty Recipes For Disaster New Adult Romance Series</u> (This series precedes "<u>Star Bright New Adult Romance Series</u>")

Trying to win a competition for best chef is cut-throat business. Kiara Sands has just won the opportunity of a lifetime. When she arrives at Fission, she has no idea just how much her life is going to change. She's immediately introduced to Jenny Foster and Robbs Martin, her competitors in the cut throat competition. The only thing Kiara finds more distracting than Robbs' hateful attitude is the handsome executive chef, Paul Weston. It doesn't help matters that Paul is quite taken by Kiara, and showers her with more attention than he gives her competitors.

<u>Torrid Exposure New Adult Romance Series</u>

April is finished with school and ready to build a career. Coming from a well-to-do family, she has decided to reboot her life completely. With family scars too deep to mend, April craves a fresh start. But the past is harder to shake than April ever would have imagined. At the center of it all is Bennett, an old family friend who is the heir to a billionaire media mogul company. Bennett and April haven't been able to stand each other since they were kids. But as the world shifts, the two of them discover the past might be the key to their future.

Devil's Advocate BBW MC New Adult Romance Series

When Kristie comes home from college, the last thing she is expecting is her world to be turned upside down by the appearance of her step-brother, Gray. Gray is rash, impulsive and breaks the law. Kristie's mom asks if she can try to befriend Gray, in hopes to get him on the straight and narrow. The plan backfires, however, as Kristie finds herself falling for Gray. Is it possible he feels the same way? The connection between them threatens to tear down everything Kristie has ever held dear.

Obsessed Bounty Hunter Romance Series

Jacqui Schneider couldn't help it. Every time the memories of her family's brutal murder haunted her, she had to escape. The only thing that could replace her sorrow was sex...and lots of it. Depressed and with no goal in sight, Jacqui continued on with her self-deprecating lifestyle until it all changed one day. Uncle Max, an old family friend, appeared unannounced. Jacqui was astonished when Uncle Max revealed a secret to her about her father. From those few words, Jacqui's world turned completely upside down. She really didn't know her own father. In fact, she didn't even know much about Uncle Max, except that he visited them for a few days at a time over the years.

Get the latest update on new releases from the author at:

https://www.carlacoxwell.com/newsletter

This book is Part One of the "Star Bright New Adult Romance Series"

Book 1

Torn between her feelings for her agent, Jon, and Rich, a charming bad boy who has ties in the movie industry, Jenny finds herself working through her own past to try to get a grip on her present. As she struggles to learn the lesson that in Hollywood not everyone is what they appear to be, Jenny tries to become a person that she can be proud of. Will she be able to find love and success in Hollywood? Or will she be dragged down by her past forever?

Book 2

Jenny finally feels that she is able to focus firmly on her future until a ghost from her past returns to ruin her present. Things are not always what they appear when dealing with rising fame. Jenny discovers love doesn't always work out the way that she plans and friends aren't always the people she thinks they are. With the walls closing in around her, will Jenny be able to face the fear head on, or will she merely sink and drown under the waves?

Book 3

Jenny finds herself lost in Hollywood, her personal life open to tabloid drama. She has fallen into the clutches of Rich, a man who wants nothing else from her but to ride her coat tails to fame and fortune. With Rich blackmailing her, Jenny feels her grasp on her own life fading.

Book 4

Time is running out for Jenny's chance of getting rid of Rich, her blackmailer. While working out a plan to escape his clutch, she uncovers details of his past that explain why Rich is the man that he is today. As she navigates her life and strives to leave her fear in the past, will she lose everything she has worked hard to achieve? Will Rich forever have control over her or will Jenny break free and come into her own?

A New Adult Romance Series

Star Bright

Book One

By Carla Coxwell

Copyright Revelry Publishing 2015

Table of Contents

Chapter One

THE SUNLIGHT creeps into my room. I groan and turn my head the other direction, trying to sleep through it. The last thing I feel like doing is getting up this morning. I never want to get up again. Everything I've done for the last few months has been robotic.

The holiday season is usually my favorite time of year. There is nothing I love more than browsing around the shops, looking for the best things to buy for my parents and friends.

That was before everything in my life went to hell. Now the thought of seeing anyone or even shopping makes me want to go back to sleep for the rest of the day.

Maggie… my daughter…

This would have been her first Christmas.

The thought comes to me quickly, before I can attempt to stop it. I try to stop all thoughts of her. Yet all it does is drive me into the pit of despair even faster. If I start thinking about her now, I will never get out of bed. I tell myself I will handle this morning the way I handle every other morning – with baby steps.

Open my eyes. It sounds ridiculous to make that a step but when I tell myself baby steps, I truly mean baby steps. If I think of what to do all at once – get up, shower, make coffee – it is all so overwhelming that I don't want to leave my bed.

The baby steps continue. Get out of bed. Walk to the bathroom. Brush my teeth. Open the shower door. Depression makes even the thought of getting in the shower to wash, only to do it all over again tomorrow, seem idiotic.

After my shower, I decide to go grocery shopping. I remember coming home last night and not finding anything substantial to eat. Instead I ate three slices of bread and went to bed. My stomach is growling loudly at me, demanding something decent to eat.

I slip on an oversized long-sleeved T-shirt and a pair of baggy jeans. Gone are the times when I cared about what I looked like. I don't want anyone to notice me ever again. It is safe to be by myself. I tell myself I can handle being alone.

Before I leave, I check my bank account on my phone. My savings are dwindling. I need to get a job. This can't last forever. When I quit my job, I figured something else would fall into my lap. But it's hard to have things fall in your lap when you never leave your bed. *I'm becoming pathetic.* I grab my purse and head out into the chilly morning.

A thin layer of snow covers the ground. The sun has now retreated behind a mass of gray clouds. They threaten a heavy snowfall. I wouldn't mind if it snowed everyone in. Sadly, Netflix is my new best friend.

The grocery store is brimming with families with their kids in tow, out of school for the holidays. I curse myself for not thinking of this before I left my apartment this morning. I wander around blindly, my list in hand, as my gaze falls on the kids around me. My heart beats quickly in my chest and my skin feels numb. All I want is to take Maggie's hand and walk through the store with her. I would kill to see her try to grab something off the shelf or plead with me to get her a doll in the small toy section.

Instead I am alone, a panic attack blooming on the brink. What is my trigger exactly? Happy kids? Couples who look down at their children and beam? I feel stupid as I park my basket in a random aisle and bolt into the restroom, which is thankfully empty. I go into one of the stalls then close my eyes tightly.

I can't live like this forever. Every time I decide to leave the house, I find myself overwhelmed by people or past memories. Everything seems to be trying to get my attention, telling me that my old dreams have died and I am letting life pass me by.

I have done things in my life that I am not proud of. I have terrible taste in men. I have a habit of only being attracted to assholes or drunks and I have had no issues cheating on people to be with someone else.

My skin feels hot and itchy as I try to avoid the panic attack that will knock me over. I focus on my breathing.

I am here. I am here. I am here.

I am nowhere else. What I have done in the past is in the past. I can't get Maggie back. I won't get Paul back after what I've done to him. I even feel like I deserve what Robbs has done to me.

Focusing on my breathing and repeating my mantra helps slow my heart rate down. I am glad no one else has come into the bathroom. The last thing I need is someone else thinking I am crazy.

After ten minutes, I am able to leave the stall. I splash some water on my face and look in the mirror. I hardly recognize myself. I have let myself go. I have to get a handle on my life but I have no idea how to do so. I have been hoping a sign will come to let me know what to do next. But what if that is just an excuse to give myself a pass on my shitty behavior? What if this is the sign – almost having a panic attack in a supermarket over happy children?

I leave the restroom, ready to get my grocery shopping done without further incident. By the time I leave the supermarket, I am feeling grounded again. Sometimes my head gets the best of me. I decide I'll brush it from my mind and go get a coffee. I haven't bought anything frozen, so I don't need to get home right away. My inner chef refuses to die, so the thought of making a frozen meal still does not appeal to me, even with how depressed I am.

It has been a while since I have treated myself to an overpriced iced coffee. But today is quickly becoming a day that is unlike the others so I head into the coffee shop, trying to ignore the small crowd standing in line to wait. I find myself lost in thought at the menu, which seems to have doubled in items since the last time I was here.

Someone taps on my shoulder, and I nearly jump out of my skin. I take a deep breath and turn around, fearing who it will be.

"I knew it was you! I wasn't 100 percent sure, but I just had to see!"

"Kathy?" I reply, my eyes widening.

Kathy smiles a toothy grin back at me. "Jenny! It's been so long!"

"It really has," I reply and then stiffen in surprise when she brings me in for a hug.

I haven't seen Kathy since high school. We took English class together our junior and senior year. We really mostly just slacked off or talked shit about the different people in class. We probably could have been in AP English but instead had opted for the regular class. Despite the fact that both of us had been lazy about school, at least Kathy was involved in drama club. I had watched her in the school play every Christmas. They were always terrible. I vividly remember the crazy drama teacher to this day and the fact that she never did a run through of her own work. The plays always ended up being over three hours long.

Near the end of senior year, Kathy and I had a falling out. She'd dated a guy she knew I had liked.

Back then, that had been enough to end the friendship. We had lost touch. But now, instead of feeling dread at a social interaction, I feel relief. Here is someone who has no idea about what I have gone through with Kiara, Robbs or Paul. She doesn't know about Maggie either.

The relief of knowing I'm not going to have to answer uncomfortable questions makes me feel more warmly towards her than anyone else recently.

"How have you been?" she asks me.

I am cut off before I can reply because I am next in line. I order something with white chocolate, and Kathy orders something overly complicated. Before I know it, I am sitting across from her in a little table in the back of the shop. Her hair is up in a slick ponytail and her makeup looks as if it had taken hours to do. She is wearing an outfit that fits her like a glove. She looks absolutely stunning. Kathy was always a bit of a wallflower in social situations in the past. She only came alive in the terrible plays. But now it looks as if the sun is shining down directly on her.

"So, tell me what has been going on with you?" I prompt, not wanting to start the discussion with me going first.

"Oh, nothing in this boring old town. I'm planning on moving, actually."

My heart drops, which I know is stupid. I have just met her after years of no contact. Already I have apparently leapt ahead to having a friend here, someone

I could reconnect with. The fact Kathy is moving shuts the door firmly in my face.

"Where are you moving to?"

"Hollywood!" Her eyes light up as she takes a sip of her coffee. "I got a new agent, and we agreed trying to bounce around for work in this town is a bad idea. Better to move to the heart of it. Just pack up and leave."

Just pack up and leave. The words roll across my brain. I have a mental image of packing up and just leaving. Somewhere where no one knows me. Paris. Hong Kong. London. It doesn't matter. Somewhere no one will see me or know my past.

"Hollywood, wow," I breathe, thinking of how the city never sleeps and there are always things to do. "That sounds amazing, really. So you're going for the big time then, huh?"

Kathy nods. "Sure am. I had one foot in my old world living here and another in Hollywood. But you can't have both. I realized you have to pick a world and stay in it. But why would I stay in the old world when I know for a fact that it doesn't make me happy?"

Her words resonate with me. I take a sip of my own coffee to stall for time before I respond. I don't want to say anything stupid. I am worried I'll look weird if I start to spill my heart out to Kathy. But her words are burrowing into my chest, heading toward my heart. *A foot in one world and a foot in another world.*

"What about you?" Kathy asks. "What are you up to?"

Lie. Make something up. Tell her you volunteer at the library or something. I try to take in a long deep breath only to let out a strange choked noise.

"Nothing," I reply, my voice strange and high pitched. "I'm not doing anything."

Chapter Two

I can't believe it. I feel like an ass. Here I am, literally blubbering about my life to a friend I haven't spoken to since high school. I was so thrilled at someone not knowing the baggage in my life. Yet for some reason Kathy asking me how I am doing and realizing I can tell someone who was on the outside about what I had gone through was enough for me to spill my guts.

I spew up the entire story. Kiara. Working as a server. Being with Paul and Robbs. Losing my baby and what Robbs did. By the time I finish, the ice in my coffee has melted, making it undrinkable. Some people are glancing over at me, as if trying to figure out why a woman is crying in the middle of the coffee shop.

To Kathy's credit, she didn't once look overwhelmed or put off by my sudden emotional outburst. She lets me talk without interrupting or getting up and walking off. How much of that is due to being polite and how much of that is because of how much she cares, I don't know. All I know is when I finally finish my tale of woe, I feel as if a giant bubble has burst inside of me. The bubble of negativity that I have been holding inside of me for what felt like ages is now gone.

However, I feel mortified. I can't believe I just blurted everything out to someone who is practically a stranger. I rub my eyes swiftly to stop more tears from coming.

"I am *so* sorry," I say, taking in a shuddering breath. "Oh my god, this is so… I can't believe… I'm so sorry." I bury my face into my hands and try to calm my sobbing.

But Kathy shakes her head, her brown eyes wide with concern. "No, Jenny, it's okay. You needed to talk. To really talk, by the looks of it. And what you told me – what you've gone through – makes my last rough period look like a vacation."

I feel ashamed. The last thing I want to do is trivialize anything someone else has gone through with my own bullshit. I open my mouth to say as much but Kathy speaks first.

"Listen, I need a roommate. I have the apartment I want all set up, but I can only live alone for about three months before I run out of savings. I was going to look for a roommate once I got to Hollywood, but why don't you come with me?"

I freeze. What she is suggesting is the last thing I expected her to say.

"No, no," I reply, shaking my head. "I couldn't possibly."

"Why not?" Kathy presses. "You said yourself that there's nothing left for you here. That's how I feel about living here too. Plus the amount of money I was spending on flying to Hollywood and back was stupid. Two different worlds, remember? That's what's going on with you, too. You have a world where you're stuck in the past and a new one that I'm offering you. Come to Hollywood. Experience the world with me. You said yourself you don't want to be a chef anymore, so come on."

I suddenly feel in over my head. This all sounds too good to be true. I stand up suddenly, wanting nothing more than to get out of here.

"I need to go. Let me think about it, okay? When do you leave?"

"This Friday. Let me give you my number."

I log her number into my phone and then bolt, giving her a quick wave. Once I get back outside, the cold air smacks me in the face. I feel stupid for blurting everything out like that. There is no way Kathy could honestly mean for me to come with her, right? But as I get in my car, I remember the look on her face when she asked me. She truly did mean it.

But should I take her up on it?

That evening, the snow kicks up. The threatening gray skies finally open up. The white flakes come down heavily, covering everything like a blanket as I curl up on the couch watching TV. For the first time in ages, I make hot chocolate and do several loads of laundry.

That, plus the grocery shopping and my conversation with Kathy, means this day has been one of the most productive I have had in ages.

It could be because the entire time I have been thinking about what Kathy has offered - moving to Hollywood. What would I do there? Wait on tables yet again? I don't want to get back in the same business, but my experience in other areas is lacking.

But haven't I been wishing about packing up and going where no one knows who I am? And now I have the option but I'm stumbling. I am stalling and trying to find a reason to say no. Kathy is right. I am afraid of moving forward. That and the thought of my dwindling savings makes me call her later that evening before bed.

"Did I wake you?" I blurt out before Kathy can even fully answer "Hello?". I cringe to myself at how I seem to have lost all proper manners lately.

"No, I'm usually up super late. What's up?"

"I was thinking… about your offer… the one to move to Hollywood." I am stalling, suddenly feeling unsure again.

"Listen, I know it was a lot to spring on you. I get like that sometimes, just so full of crazy ideas that I spew them out without thinking them all the way through. Of course you have a life here that you need to tend to. It'd be insane to expect you to just drop everything and go."

My heart falls. Is she retracting her offer? I suddenly realize that I *want* to go. That is what I truly want. Anything else is the fear talking, trying to hold me back in my depressive slump that I call my life.

"But," Kathy goes on, oblivious to my inner dialogue, "I still think you should consider it. I can give you the number to my old agent. He's excellent, but he had to drop off some clients because of a family emergency. I volunteered to be one and then just hopped to another agent he recommended because I didn't feel like waiting. I just don't want you to think I'm giving you someone shitty."

"An agent?" I reply, stumbling over my words. "Why would I need an agent?"

"You don't want to go after the dream of being a chef anymore. So why not try getting into show business?"

I swallow my laughter. I know Kathy is being serious. I don't want to seem as if I am pissing all over her idea. But honestly - acting? How can she be serious? I don't know the first thing about acting. I have a mental image of me in a commercial for a feminine hygiene product, jumping into the air to hit a volleyball or strolling along the beach, a big smile plastered on my face because of my brand of tampon.

"Kathy, I don't think I need an agent." I hope I don't sound like that was the craziest idea I have ever heard.

"You won't get anywhere without an agent, Jenny, trust me. Anyone who doesn't have one is filming low budget horror movies in ten-minute segments 'cause they can't afford filming permits anywhere." Something in her tone makes me think that she has had experience in this as she goes on. "Anyway, Jon is great. I'll give you his number."

"No, Kathy, I mean that I don't think acting is for me. I don't know the first thing about acting. I've never done that for a second in my life."

"Oh. Well listen, it could be a talent you don't even know you have! Think of it as an adventure!"

An adventure. I allow the words to sink into my head. If I am going to Hollywood, then why not go all the way? I have been slumping around here, fending off panic attacks over happy children and thinking about Robbs and Paul. I need to reinvent myself desperately. And even if acting turns out not to be my thing, it's Hollywood. I can find something else to do.

"Okay," I say. "Sounds good. Let's do this."

Kathy squeals, sounding relieved at having found a roommate already. "Great! That's great! I'll text you the information for the place I'm renting. I'll be leaving before you, but that's okay. I'll get everything set up. You just get things wrapped up on your end."

We talk a little more before I hang up the phone. I suddenly feel exhausted. Was it really this morning I had woken up, using baby steps to get myself into the shower? Now I'm moving to Hollywood. I look out the window.

Everything is going to change. Am I ready to reinvent myself?

Chapter Three

My heart is pounding in my chest. The taxi driver is ignoring me, lost in whatever terrible music he's listening to. I turn back to watch my apartment become smaller and smaller. Has it really only been two weeks since Kathy made me the offer to come with her to Hollywood?

I had to quickly sell my car. Settled for much less than what it was actually worth which bummed me out. The cost of living in Hollywood is much higher than here, and I needed the cash, especially since I have been using my savings to laze around. I had to pay a fee to end my lease early. Lastly, I told everyone on Christmas that I was leaving.

It hadn't gone as well as I would have liked it to. I understand it all seemed sudden. My family is worried I am making a rash decision and am having a lapse of lucid judgement. My words had failed me when I tried to explain to them that I need to get out of here and start somewhere new.

I sold everything I could and packed up my clothes. Before I know it, I'm riding toward the airport. Kathy has been there for a week already and tells me that her old agent, Jon, is waiting for my call.

That is something I haven't told anyone else – the possibility of acting. I know that everyone will shoot it down and with good reason. I have spent a ridiculous amount of time Googling stuff about acting. The chances of anything coming of this are slim to none. My previous notion of landing a tampon commercial is dreaming too high. I will be lucky if I get an audition.

I told Kathy as much, but she brushed off my concerns. She is overly positive for someone who, from what I can gather, has gotten only tiny roles here and there in commercials and bad movies. But I don't want to suddenly piss on her parade since we're going to be roommates and she'll be my only friend in an unfamiliar city.

By the time the taxi arrives at the airport, I have worked myself up in a frenzy. Part of me wants to stay in the taxi and turn back around, back to my apartment. Call the whole idea off. But I have nowhere to live here now. If I don't head to Hollywood, I'll just be homeless and jobless.

After spending what feels like an eternity getting through security and waiting for the plane, I finally locate my seat. I plop down into the window seat, hoping whoever sits next to me won't feel like talking. I decide I'll put on headphones and zone out with an inflight movie. I wish I brought something to read as well in case the movie options are horrible.

I press my head against the airplane window, which is cold to the touch. I am leaving, going to Hollywood and starting over. I shut my eyes and take in a deep breath. Will it be possible to move on from my past? To not wake up in the middle of the night and feel haunted by what had happened to Maggie?

All I can do is move forward and find out for myself.

By the time I finally get to Hollywood, I'm feeling a strange mix of exhaustion and exhilaration. Every nerve in my body hums. I desperately want a shower. My face is glued to the window as we land. I am finally here.

Kathy is waiting for me by the baggage claim. She runs over to me, dressed as if she is going to a business meeting. Her hair is up in a bun, and she wears a dark brown pantsuit with a fabulous necklace. I feel frumpy in my sweatshirt and yoga pants. Everyone around me is dressed to the nines in clothes that I wish I owned. *Investing in a new wardrobe is something I hadn't considered.* It is true. Somehow in all of my planning, the fact that I am moving to Hollywood, where the young and rich come to play, had fallen out of my head.

"Hey!" Kathy shouts. "How was the flight?"

"Long. The layover felt even longer. But I'm here now! I could totally use a shower."

"Great. Let's get your stuff, and you can finally see your new home!"

Before I know it, we have my luggage and are stepping outside. I am bowled over by how humid it is.

Suddenly I realize that I am the only person wearing a sweatshirt in the entire baggage claim. Now I understand why. I yank it off, revealing a baggy T-shirt I had thrown on in the last second before leaving.

I get in Kathy's car, and we zip out of the airport, heading toward her – no, *our* – new place.

"I have the apartment unpacked and set up but if you find you need anything we can just run out and buy it. I know you were bummed about selling your car, but feel free to use mine. I like to walk around Hollywood anyway, so you can use it unless I have an audition. You should call Jon tonight, too. He wants to get the ball rolling with you ASAP." Her tone is clipped and sharp, as if she has a mental list in her mind a mile long.

I nod mutely, still on sensory overload as we pull off the highway and into Hollywood. I look outside my window at all the palm trees. Even more people. The sky is a bright blue, as if we are in a marble. The buildings are tall, gleaming in the sunlight. Everything I look at makes it clear I am a far cry from back home.

"It's overwhelming when you first get here," Kathy says, clearly making note of my expression. "But you'll love it, truly."

I tear my eyes away from someone playing their guitar on a street corner and look at her. "Thanks for… all of this."

"Don't mention it. It isn't a problem. It works out for me too, since I needed a roommate."

"Are you nervous about living here full time?"

Kathy shakes her head as we hit traffic. "Nah. I'll never make it if I don't make the full jump."

"Does this old agent of yours…"

"Jon."

"Right, Jon. Does he know I've never acted a day in my life?"

"He's looking for new blood, Jenny. Someone with potential. That's you. You just have to unlock it in yourself."

I look back outside the window as we inch forward. *Unlock it myself.* I used to be able to do that. I used to be confident and look where it got me. *No*, I tell myself firmly, brushing thoughts of the past away. I am not going to fall down that hole. Not here.

It feels like it takes ages to get to the apartment. The traffic is unreal. There is even traffic on the smaller roads. It isn't until she makes a few more turns that the roads are clear of traffic and we are driving at a normal speed.

"Is it always like that?"

"The traffic?"

I nod. "Yeah, it's pretty brutal."

"Usually always bad, especially on weekdays. If you're going anywhere, make sure you factor in the traffic and learn to be patient."

I open my mouth to reply when we turn down another side street and pull into an apartment complex. It is a far cry from the luxurious high rise apartments that I saw back in the heart of the city. This apartment complex is four floors and looks as if the last time someone cleaned the roof was some time in the last century. One of the apartments on the bottom floor has a window that has been patched together with duct tape. The whole complex looks depressed, as if everyone who lives here has given up on their dreams.

"I know what it looks like."

I glance at Kathy and realize I must look horrified. I quickly shake my head.

"No, no, it looks fine," I lie. "Really."

I can tell Kathy doesn't believe me. The place looks like a dump. But I don't want to complain about the place we both are living in. I don't want to sound spoiled. So we get out of the car and grab my things. As we get closer to the complex, I can see that it looks even worse up close. The sidewalks are cracked and badly in need of some repairs. The paint on the doors is faded and chipped. It looks as if the entire complex let out one long sigh and then just gave up.

We tug my luggage up to the third floor. I am panting by the time we walk down the hallway. The staircase is rusted and creaks, which makes me paranoid enough to lean against the bannister as I wait for Kathy to unlock the front door. The last thing I need is to fall and break my neck. The apartment is facing the sad little parking lot and a taco shop across the street. No, it is not the height of glamor but at least tacos are close by.

Kathy gets the door open, and I yank my luggage in after her, closing the door with my foot. Then I look up to see where I am now living.

The living room is small and a little cramped but Kathy has clearly done her best to make it look "homey". The floor is tile but she has tossed down a deep red area rug to try to soften the room. A TV is against the wall. The couch has some throw pillows on it. Pictures of flowers hang on the wall. I am happy they aren't of her and her friends. I don't want to feel the urge to try to tack up old photos of my past so I don't look so pathetic.

Off to the left, I can see an even smaller dining area, with a table and two chairs. I can't see the kitchen, but my guess is it will be incredibly small as well.

"It's nice," I lie and plaster a smile on my face. "Where is my room?"

"Just off by the kitchen. That's one of the reasons I liked this floor plan so much. We each have our own space."

I trail after her. As I figured, the kitchen can barely fit the two of us. There is a hallway in between the dining room and kitchen. The bathroom is there and next to the bathroom is my room.

I step inside. Any silly bummed out feelings I have been having over the fact I don't have my own personal bathroom is wiped away by another concern.

"Wow," I breathe. "It's … quaint."

Microscopic is the actual word that jumped into my head but I brush it aside. My bed, which I have shipped ahead of time, takes up almost the entire room. It is a good thing I barely brought anything from my old apartment. It won't fit. I open the closet and examine how little space I have there as well. My mood darkens. This place is a fucking dollhouse. I should have asked for the master bedroom.

"I know it's small. But for our budget, it's the best we could get. And to be honest, it really isn't that bad. Yeah, it's a little out of the way and cramped, but we won't really be here much. We're going to be hitting the pavement and making our dreams come true!"

I bite my bottom lip, looking outside the window. I have a fantastic view of the parking lot and the taco shop. If I squint, I can see the high rises on the horizon. I could always stare at them and pretend that I was rich.

I know Kathy is waiting for me to tell her how I feel. But complaining about what she has managed to pull together, and even putting me in contact with her old agent on top of it, makes me feel like a bitch. She is right. Hollywood is expensive.

"It will take some getting used to. But you're right! This is Hollywood! I hope we won't be spending all day inside."

Kathy smiles, looking relieved. She turns to go get the rest of the suitcases, and I find myself staring back out the window. The self-doubt I felt on the airplane is back in full force. I shake my head, trying to clear my thoughts. At least now I have motivation not to lie around the apartment all day.

Chapter Four

Sleep doesn't come easily. Even though I am exhausted and in bed at eight o'clock because of the time difference, I end up just lying there. Tomorrow, I have plans to call Jon and see if he would be interested in representing me. A lot hinges on this meeting. If he declines, I have to triple my efforts to find a job. Kathy might be able to pay the bills with her acting alone, but I still need another job on top of looking for auditions.

The fear that I haven't thought this all the way through is still gnawing at me. Should I have looked for a job first? What if I don't find any work? In the end, I tell myself to stop overthinking it and focus on my breathing until I calm down and fall asleep.

When I open my eyes in the morning, the first sight is a different ceiling that isn't one I'm used to seeing. The cheap blinds that came with the room offer almost no protection from the sun. I make a mental note to buy better ones when I can. After yanking out clean clothes from my suitcase and stumbling into the bathroom, I manage to get into the shower.

There is a note on the counter when I get out of the shower from Kathy, saying she is running out to get some items for the apartment and she'll be back soon. I relax slightly. For some reason it makes me nervous to call Jon when she is around. It sounds silly, but I want to make this call alone.

"Hello, this is Jon," he says, answering on the first ring.

I clutch my phone tightly. I had thought the number was for his office, not his personal cell phone. For some reason, I feel thrown off. I had planned to put on my formal voice when I spoke to the receptionist but now find myself stumbling.

"Uh … hi? Hi! This is Jenny," I stumble through, cringing. "Kathy's friend," I add lamely.

"Oh! Hey, there." Jon's voice is smooth, as if he deals with idiots like me on a daily basis. "Kathy said you would be calling me soon."

"Yeah, I got in yesterday. Hope it isn't too late to discuss anything."

He is in his car, I can hear his AC blasting in the background. "No, not at all. Kathy was a great client. It was a shame to lose her, but family things just came up. I had to transfer a lot of clients."

"That sucks." I hate how boring I sound.

"Anyway, I have an opening today at around three. Last minute cancel. Do you think you could make it?"

I was hoping for tomorrow, honestly, if only to try to prepare myself mentally a bit more. But there is no way to say no to this. If I want to learn how to be a fully functioning human being again, throwing myself into things is going to be the best bet.

"Sounds great."

"See you then, Jenny."

We hang up, and I stare at the phone. *See you then, Jenny.* I like the way my name rolls off his tongue. He could do voice overs. I shake my head and shoot Kathy a text. Now it is time to get ready.

We hit traffic again. When Kathy had wanted to leave almost an hour early to get somewhere twenty minutes away, according to my phone's GPS, I had thought she was pulling my leg. But no, she is right, as usual. I should learn to stop doubting her when it comes to the traffic in Hollywood.

Kathy peppers me with advice and it makes my head feel crowded. I know she means well, but it is just making my nerves worse. I am grateful for her help with the outfit though. While I don't look as well dressed as most people in the city, at least I don't look like I did when I got off the plane yesterday.

"Jon is very direct," Kathy is saying to me and I try to focus on her as we hit another red light. "Some people can find it off putting, but I found it helpful."

"Why didn't you just go back to him when his family emergency was done?"

Something flickers across Kathy's face – it is so quick that I figure I must have imagined it because in the next second, she is smiling. "I had signed on with this new agent and it was just too much of a hassle to move back."

I nod, looking outside the window again. I miss my own car. I wish I hadn't had to sell it. *When you have enough money,* I promise myself, although I don't know when that will actually be. I run my fingers over my skirt, trying to recite Kathy's advice to me. As if sensing my nerves, she falls silent, too.

We pull up into an office building that looks about a hundred years old. It is only four floors. For some reason, I was imagining a skyscraper, housing celebrities and models with maybe even some paparazzi surrounding it.

"You were expecting something else, right?" Kathy says, a smile on her face.

"Honestly, yeah. Something a bit more glamorous." Where was the glamor in this city anyway?

"Most agents have plain boring offices like this."

I get out of the car. I wonder what else in Hollywood isn't going to be how I expected it. I guess a lot. I take a deep breath and follow Kathy into the main floor. We don't stop at the desk and instead go straight toward the elevator.

"Third floor," she says to me as I step inside.

"You're not coming with me?" I blurt nervously.

"Nah, I'll wait for you though. There's a coffee shop next door. Good luck!"

I was going to protest and tell her I need the support but before I get the chance, she reaches into the elevator and presses the button. The doors glide shut and the elevator is lifting upward. Is it stupid to wish Kathy had come with me? I guess so. But I still would feel better. Even with all her advice, it would be good to have her with me. *I have to do this alone,* I tell myself as the elevator doors open to the third floor.

I walk into a modern waiting area. There is a fish tank off to one side and lots of windows. A woman sits at a desk, the sound of her long nails clicking as she types. I walk over to her and clear my throat. She stops typing and smiles. Her teeth are so white, they're practically blinding, especially in contrast to her California-bronzed complexion. Her nails are a neon pink. She looks as though she could be an actress herself.

"Let me guess," she trills. "You must be Jenny."

"Yes," I clear my throat again, "I am."

"Have a seat. I'll let Jon know you are here. It shouldn't be long."

I nod and sit down on one of the chairs. I pull out my cellphone and start to fiddle with it. I can't believe how nervous I feel. I really want this guy to agree to represent me. I want to turn over a new leaf and start a career that no one would expect from me. This is my best shot. I take a deep breath and exhale slowly. My nerves lessen a little. I can't blow this. I have to be on my A game.

"Jenny?" I look up at the sound of my name. "Jon will see you now."

I stand up and follow the assistant down a small hallway. She stops at the door at the very end, smiles at me, and opens it. I step inside slowly. The office is as modern as the waiting room. The view is of the parking lot. A man turns around in his desk chair and smiles at me.

"Jenny, welcome," he says as he stands up and walks over to me.

My throat goes dry. I am knocked over by how handsome Jon is. I have heard that people in Hollywood are more attractive than everyone else. I had brushed that off as due to Botox and any other crazy anti-aging stuff famous people went through. But Jon is gorgeous. His black hair is slightly messy and falls into his eyes a little. His suit is well tailored and clings in all the right spots to make it obvious there are tight muscles underneath. *Oh no, he's hot!*

He holds out his hand to shake. His smile is bright and his teeth whiter than I ever thought possible.

I shake his hand. An electric shock goes through me. I hope I don't look like a deer caught in headlights. All the thoughts have emptied out of my head. His brown eyes remind me of warm coffee as I take a seat across from his desk. I find myself automatically checking for a wedding ring. No ring. *Stop it, you want this guy to represent you. You aren't supposed to find him hot.* It figures that the first man I find attractive in ages turns out to be my potential agent.

"It's nice to finally meet you," I manage to say.

"Same. Kathy has told me a lot about you. Do you want coffee or water to drink?"

I ask for water, and he goes over to a small minifridge in the corner of his office.

"Kathy said you're great. Said you helped her a lot before you had to drop some clients due to a family emergency." I cut myself off, hoping I haven't said too much.

Jon has gone still over by the fridge, as if I have caught him off guard. "Right. Luckily the family emergency is all squared away now."

"Great!" I chirp, my nerves getting the better of me.

Jon hands me a bottle of water and sits back down, opening his own. "Kathy say anything else?"

I take a sip of the water and shake my head. "Just that you are great at what you do."

Jon smiles and my knees go weak. I'm glad I'm sitting down.

"Well, she mentioned you didn't have any experience in acting, is that correct?"

I think about mentioning a fourth-grade play where I had been Merlin but decide against it. "That's right. Is that okay?"

"It will take a little longer to get you rolling but not a big deal. Most people who come by have a head shot and maybe a portfolio."

"Head shot?" I repeat stupidly.

"Just a picture of you that casting directors can use to see if you'd fit the part."

"I'm going to guess a selfie from last time I went to the beach wouldn't count."

Jon laughs. It sounds like music and I find myself smiling in return, feeling more relaxed.

"No, but we can get you set up with a photographer. You don't have a portfolio yet either, so we'll have to start off small. Get some audition demos out there. Do you have any acting training at all?"

"No. But I can thrill casting directors with tales of how I used to be in the restaurant business. I can even tell them how to make a great salad."

Jon smiles again. Maybe I am imagining it, but it feels as if his eyes rest on me for a few extra seconds before he looks at his computer.

"I think you'll do great on some test shots and an audition tape. I'll have to schedule you to come back so we can get everything all set up."

My heart skips a beat. "Does this mean that…?"

"I'll represent you. I'll have my assistant draw up a contract for you to review. Just sign it and bring it back next time we meet up."

I feel as if my heart is constricting. "Are you sure you want to sign me? I have nothing to offer." I am about to blow this. I bite my tongue to shut myself up.

"Okay, first lesson – try not to say that to anyone else." Jon laughs. "I know raw talent when I see it, Jenny."

Again, I like the way my name sounds from his mouth. I stand up as he does.

"I'm about to head out for the day," he says. "Why don't I walk you downstairs?"

I agree and we leave his office together after his assistant gives me a contract to sign. I grip it tightly in my hands, afraid that if I let it go it will fly away. In the elevator, I can smell Jon's cologne. It is subtle but makes my head swim. I try not to check him out.

"You and Kathy are roommates, right?" he says as the doors slide shut.

I nod. "That's right. Sort of whirlwind how it all happened but I wanted to get out of where I was living."

Jon looks at me, and I can feel goose bumps spring up along my skin, "You came to the perfect city to reinvent yourself then."

The elevator doors open, and we step out together into the lobby.

"Have you lived here long?" I ask Jon, wanting to keep the conversation going.

"Yes, a while now," he replies. "But I couldn't imagine going back to where I was before."

I was going to respond when I see Kathy heading over to me. I give her a wave, but she falters when she sees Jon.

"Hey," Kathy says as she walks up to us. "I finished grabbing what I needed at the store across the street so I was going to wait for you."

"I'm all done. Jon is going to represent me," I reply, beaming.

Kathy smiles, but it looks forced. Jon suddenly looks at his watch and then back at me.

"I have to head out. Have somewhere to be. See you later. Nice seeing you, Kathy."

Jon leaves us and heads toward his car. I watch him go, frowning. That seems sudden. I don't quite understand what has happened. I turn to look at Kathy, who is watching him leave. I close my mouth, deciding not to tell her about my meeting. She has a funny look on her face.

As if sensing me watching her, she turns to look back at me and forces a smile. "Want to grab a coffee? Tell me all about it?"

Maybe I just imagined it.

Chapter Five

That night, I can't sleep again. This time it isn't the fact I live in a dollhouse that is bothering me. Jon has called me to ask if I can come in tomorrow to get a head shot taken. He has been able to call in a favor so I can even get it done for free. *Is he this nice to all his clients?*

I want to ask Kathy, but after seeing how weird the two of them had been with each other, I decide against it. Maybe I am imagining it, but it feels as if there is some awkward tension between the two of them. Kathy had dropped me off and told me she was meeting some friends for dinner, so I didn't get to ask. Would I ask if I was able to?

Jon's voice on the phone gave me goose bumps again. It is naïve to think that he is being nice to me because we have some sort of connection. There is no connection – I just want to jump his bones. I sigh and roll over, covering my face with my pillow. In the distance, I can hear sirens. A few apartments down, I can sometimes hear people yelling. Not a dream home by any means.

Somewhere in this city is a nightlife that entire movies are based off of. Movie stars with no concerns are getting VIP bottle service and talking about their next blockbuster movie. There is no way that can be me, right?

Do agents say they see potential in all their clients or only when they truly mean it? It doesn't help that Jon is so attractive. There is absolutely no way I can violate our professional relationship in hopes for a date. I probably just need to get laid.

I finally fall asleep. I dream of my daughter. I wake up in the morning in a cold sweat.

"I want you to look as if you are gazing out in the horizon at your destiny."

"What?" I reply as the photographer snaps photos. "Is my destiny some tangible thing I can hold?"

We are thirty minutes into trying to get a decent head shot of me, and I am feeling over it. The photographer's directions for each picture are growing increasingly vague, and I feel out of my element. I had thought the entire thing was going to be quick, like having a high school photo taken.

Unfortunately, I was wrong. Jon has gotten a woman to do my makeup and hair. I feel unlike myself, as if I can be anyone I want to be. However, the photographer's ridiculous instructions are making me hyperaware of everything.

"Let's take five," he finally says, lowering his camera. "Your aura is all wrong."

"What the fuck is an aura?" I mumble to myself through clenched teeth.

Jon walks over. He is dressed casually compared to yesterday and has a bemused expression on his face. My heart does a flip.

"Jon, where did you find this guy?" I whisper.

"I called in a favor. He normally doesn't do head shots."

"You think?"

Jon laughs. "He's trying to make it big. He'll take what he can. We're going to get head shots plus some other photos I can use, too. It's a win-win, even if it doesn't feel like it."

"It does not feel like it."

"Come on, let's grab a coffee."

I follow him over to the small table that has been set up with some food. The guy who is doing the lighting is cramming a donut in his mouth as he talks on his phone. The makeup artist is gossiping to the photographer about seeing a celebrity at some club named Underwater Nosh last night. What a name.

I borrowed Kathy's car to get here. It took about an hour to get twenty minutes to the tiny studio. I had asked her if she wanted me to take a cab but she refused. I am pretty sure she is hung over from wherever she went to last night.

Lost in thought, I don't even hear people greet the man who has just come in. I pour myself my coffee, trying to shake off my tired state. I really need to sleep better. If I get regular acting jobs, I might have to get up at 4 a.m.

"Rich, I didn't expect to see you here," Jon says, although his tone sounds stiff.

"I heard someone was using my studio today for some new talent and I wanted to scope it out for myself."

"Did you." Jon replies. It is meant to be a question but comes out more like a tone of annoyance.

I realize just then that I am the "talent" and turn around to see who owns the studio. I am facing another handsome man. Is there any other kind in Hollywood? He is the polar opposite of Jon. His hair is a light blond and he wears a tan suit. His blue eyes are bright and gorgeous, reminding me of the ocean.

"I'm Rich."

"Jenny. Hi. You said you own the studio?"

We shake hands and he nods. "Yes. I own quite a few on this side of town."

"Among other things," Jon mumbles.

Rich either doesn't hear him or ignores him because he goes on, "I'm also a casting director. I used to work with Jon before we went our separate ways. You didn't tell me you had such a beautiful new client though."

I feel butterflies in my stomach. Is this guy *flirting* with me? In front of everyone? No way. He said he is a casting agent. Maybe he just likes what he sees. Maybe I'll even get lucky and he'll cast me in something.

"Jenny is new to the business but I think she has something real to offer the casting agents here. Something different."

Rich's eyes scan my body. "Looks like it."

I can feel heat rising to my cheeks. He is flirting. I open my mouth to respond when the photographer, apparently bored of hearing about Underwater Nosh, turns and claps his hands. "Back to work!"

I am back in front of the camera. Jon mumbles something in the photographer's ear, whose enthusiasm dims as he goes and gets a chair for me to sit in.

"Apparently we have enough shots for my own portfolio," he says in a low voice to me. "Sit. We'll get your head shot now."

I look over at Jon and mouth the words, "Thank you."

He winks in reply. I turn my head quickly, sitting down. He is just playing around with the wink, I tell myself, as my stomach gets butterflies again. I can feel Rich's eyes on me as well. Two good looking guys both watching me get my photo taken. It is perfect. If only I felt more confident in my poses.

It doesn't take long for the photographer to get my head shot. Apparently he cares more about building his portfolio rather than what he was actually hired to do. I can't blame him. I have gotten the head shot for free because of the favor Jon has called in. I *do* have extra photos on top of it.

Once we finish, I hesitate walking over to Jon. He seems to be in a serious conversation with Rich, who is cute and clearly interested in me. No matter how much Jon gives me the shivers and goose bumps, he is still my agent. Going after him would be foolish, given our professional relationship.

But Rich on the other hand? If he wants to flirt again, I am considering flirting back. He is super cute, after all, and focusing on a new guy might make any fantasies brewing in my head over Jon to vanish.

With all this in my mind, I decide to head over to the two of them. Jon sees me first and falls silent as Rich looks up.

"You did great," Jon says. "I'm going to get everything organized and start putting my feelers out there for an audition. I'll send you the photos, too."

"You should send her information my way, too," Rich says, his eyes still on me. "I might have something for her."

My heart thrums. "Really?"

"A beautiful thing like you? Be stupid not to."

"I'm heading out," Jon announces. "I'll talk to you later, Jenny."

I say "bye" and watch him go. Does he care about me talking to Rich or am I imagining that, like Kathy being odd?

"You looked great today."

I snap out of my thoughts to look at Rich and smile. "Thanks."

"You new in town?"

"Yes. Just moved here recently."

"How are you liking it?" He moves an inch closer to me and I feel a tingle go down my spine – something about him seems like a bad boy.

I can feel my old urges kicking up. *Bad Jenny.*

"I haven't really seen much of it," I admit, batting my eyelashes at him. "I heard the photographer and the make-up artist talking about some club named Underwater Nosh? I don't know what that is."

There is a noise behind me of someone coming back in the studio. Probably the photographer. Rich is looking directly at me, a slow smile spreading across his face.

"Underwater Nosh is the hottest club in the city right now. Highly exclusive."

"Oh," I reply. "I won't be getting in there any time soon then."

"Maybe not. Unless I take you."

My eyes widen. "You take me? Are you sure?"

"Of course. Consider it a date. I'll show you around and you can show me around."

Yes, clearly a bad boy. My type completely. *No*, I amend in my brain, *my old type*. I am not supposed to be into these sort of guys anymore. But would it really hurt seeing the hottest club in Hollywood?

"Great," I reply. "It's a date!"

Rich smiles. When I turn around, I see that it was Jon who has come into the studio again. His face is blank but it is obvious he has overheard us making plans. I snatch up my purse and head toward the bathroom, my face grows hot.

It doesn't matter. It doesn't matter. He is your agent.

Chapter Six

"Wow, Underwater Nosh? I probably couldn't even get twenty feet from the entrance," Kathy says, poking her head into my bedroom.

"Same here. It sounds so exciting. Actually seeing Hollywood, you know?"

"Rich – he used to work with Jon. If he likes you, I bet you can totally get a part."

I freeze. I am holding a dress in my hands but suddenly realize how ugly it is and toss it onto my bed. Get a part? That seems wrong somehow and is not what I am aiming for. Spurred on by what Kathy just said, I follow her to the tiny kitchen. She is making instant noodles.

"Get a part?" I echo.

"Yeah, that's right. I mean, he might think you're perfect for something and give you an audition, at the very least."

"Isn't that…" I grasp for the best word to describe it. "Cheating?"

Kathy laughs, looking at me over her shoulder. "That is not cheating, Jenny. That's Hollywood. It is all about connections, trust me. If he is really impressed with you, a part just might fall into your lap."

"That feels… wrong, somehow."

Kathy shakes her head. "It isn't wrong. It's Hollywood."

<<<>>>

I take a taxi to meet Rich at Underground Nosh. He has offered to come pick me up but I actually feel embarrassed about him seeing the apartment. If he is rich enough to get me into this club, I blanch at the thought of what he would say about where I live.

I get to the entrance of the club five minutes early. Shoving money at the taxi driver, I get out, steeling myself. The line for the club wraps around the block. It looks as if waiting to get in would take hours, if you were even allowed inside. Kathy has told me this place is the hottest of the hottest. They probably let only a few nobodies inside. I can only imagine the bribes the bouncers saw nightly.

I wait along the sidewalk for Rich. I feel under-dressed. Everyone in line looks dressed to the nines. Some people are wearing fashions that look as if they cost thousands of dollars and here they are, wearing them out on the street. In comparison, my glittery night dress seems laughable. Not for the first time, I think to myself that I need a new wardrobe.

"There you are!"

I turn around and see Rich walking over to me. My heart skips a beat. He looks so *good*. He is wearing all black, which brings out his eyes, even in the neon colors from the sign. His hair is slicked back, and he oozes bad boy charm.

"Here I am," I reply, hoping he doesn't think I look as if I have moved here from Smalltown, U.S.A.

"I've been looking for you."

Confused, I reply with, "What? Isn't this the entrance?"

Rich laughs at my question and reaches for my hand. "For the regular people."

I take his hand and he escorts me away. Everyone is eyeing us, shooting us curious looks. Some people are downright glaring, as if they know where we are going. I sure as hell don't. We round the nearest corner and walk along the side of the club and some coffee shop. Music vibrates through the walls and along the sidewalk. Even here, people mill around, smoking cigarettes, as if just hanging out near the club was enough.

"Where are we going?" I ask as we turn another corner.

He doesn't have to reply. As soon as we round another corner, we find ourselves in a smaller line. Rich hands something to me – some sort of badge on a lanyard, which I put around my neck.

"Make sure you wear this till we get in. You need this to be in line."

"A badge to get in a line?" I feel very out of my element.

"VIP entrance. Otherwise this line would look like the one up front."

"Oh, VIP." I nudge him. "Impressive."

He grins at me and my mood lightens. As nervous as I am about getting into a high-end club like this, it feels like it will be okay when he smiles at me. The music is vibrating along the walls. I am suddenly anxious to get inside.

The line moves rapidly. Before I know it, we are staring at the bouncer.

"Mr. Dawkins!" the bouncer says, shaking his hand. "Nice to see you again. Come on inside."

I mouth, "Impressive."

Rich laughs and then we step inside the club. It is clearly the coat room, but I am amazed at the detail that went into it. There are lights that mimic being underwater along the walls and even the ceiling is painted to look as if we are underwater, looking up at the sun.

We walk past the coat check, continuing further along. I take a deep breath and step onto the main floor. I keep my mouth closed, even though my eyes widen in awe at the sight in front of us. The dance floor is absolutely jammed with people. It actually looks like an ocean wave, filled with people. They dance and move against each other, lost in the ear-splitting dub step beat that is playing. It is so loud that it feels as if it is worming into my brain.

The décor of the club is five steps further than the coat room. There are patterns of moving waves near the top of the club, but this time with lights, so it appears as if it is moving. Fish dart along the walls, swimming in giant aquariums. Something about them seems off, although I can't pinpoint what.

Rich leans over to me and gets close to my ear. "Fish are robotic!"

It makes sense, I think, as I watch one of the robot fish dart in its aquarium. Way easier to maintain. Plus fish will not appreciate the vibrations from the music. They look so lifelike though. Rich takes my hand again, and we move through the crowd. People bump into me non-stop, so I stop excusing myself and just focus on making sure not to lose Rich's hand. I feel as if I let go I'll be swallowed up by the human ocean.

We pass one of the bars, which is absolutely packed. We pass it and walk up a spiral staircase toward the second floor. There is a bouncer here as well. VIP entrance and now the VIP room? Rich knows how to spoil a girl on the first date. Our passes get us past the bouncer and into the VIP area.

This isn't as crowded, although it is just as lively. The floor is translucent as if I am standing on the ocean. If I look below my feet, I see more fake fish, as well as coral reefs and even a fake lobster. Above my head, the ceiling is made to mimic the look of sky, with a fake sun shining down on us. The sky is illuminated and changes colors with the music.

Entranced, I try to soak in the rest of the VIP area. I swear that I see at least two popular singers at one table. The dance floor is crowded here as well, with dancers in cages that mimic being underwater. The effects of the water elongate their features. They glow like jellyfish in the dance cages.

Rich pulls me toward one of the smaller tables and we sit down. A waitress comes by to take our drink orders almost instantly.

"Better than trying to get a drink at the bar downstairs," Rich says to me before he orders.

The waitress then turns to me, and I find myself stumbling over my own drink order, still entranced by the club. "Do you have anything that has alcohol in it but you can't actually taste the alcohol? I'm a lightweight."

"The house drink is the Jellyfish Juice. I swear you won't taste a thing."

"Sounds great."

I watch her go, thinking that Jellyfish Juice is a corny name for a drink. I'm relieved to notice that the music is a little softer by our table so we won't have to shout at one another.

Rich looks at me. "What do you think?"

"It's uh… overwhelming," I answer nervously. "I mean, the theme is effortless. It really feels like I'm partying in the Little Mermaid's mansion or something."

Rich chuckles. "It really is breathtaking. Of course, I'm sure in a year or two this place won't be nearly as packed."

"Why is that?"

"There is always another club that comes along and piques everyone's interest. You're hot till you're not, basically."

The waitress comes back with our drinks. Mine is overly decorated with a light up jellyfish hanging off the straw. I watch her leave, wondering what it must be like to work here day in and day out.

I turn back to look at Rich. "So, you must have been here for a while now, right?"

"About eight years. Moved here right out of high school. Wanted something new. Most people who end up moving here do."

"I hear you. That's why I did, too."

"There is so much to do in the city. This place is unlike anywhere else I've ever been. I feel like I'm really making something of myself here. You will, too."

I fiddle with the straw in my drink. "Will I? The odds are against me on every level, aren't they? No experience in acting and compared to everyone else, I feel like the ugly duckling."

Rich reaches across the table and holds my hand tightly, looking in my eyes. "You are anything but the ugly duckling. You'll find your way. I'll keep my eyes peeled for anything that might suit you."

"You haven't even seen me act," I reply, not wanting to point that out so clearly but having no choice.

"Jon said he's setting you up with some casting tapes later this week."

Jon had mentioned that at the photo shoot when I had first arrived. The thought makes me nervous, and I am trying not to think about it.

"Besides," Rich goes on, "I don't mind calling in favors for my girls."

I take a sip of my drink, smiling weakly at him. Calling in favors for his girls? Plural usage, by the way. What the hell did that mean? I think back to what Kathy has said about getting an audition from this date. I know she has said that is how things worked in Hollywood but it makes me feel… dirty. He didn't think I would sleep with him for an audition, did he? *This is why you were supposed to call off bad boys.*

I clear my throat. "Girls?"

Rich waves his hand at someone, yelling hello before looking back at me. "Don't look at me like that, sweetie. Come on, finish your drink and we'll go dancing."

I smile back uncertainly and take a sip of my drink.

Once we get out on the dance floor, all my concerns fly away. It has been ages since I have let loose like this. The music swirling in my head and Rich's body pressed against mine is all I need to let go of my concerns. Everything faded – living in the dollhouse, concerns about how I feel about Jon, concerns that Rich is out of my league, and concerns about my own taste in bad boys – go to the backdrop as we dance crazily together on the floor. It really does feel like I am dancing underwater.

We leave the club at close to two a.m. Too tired to take a taxi, I agree for Rich to drive me home. He pulls in front of my apartment complex but luckily doesn't say anything about how rundown it looks. Instead, he gets out of the car to walk me to the front door.

I wonder if he is going to try to kiss me. Dancing with Rich had been very sensual. We had lost ourselves to the music. It has been a long time since I have been with someone who was so good at dancing. His hands on my hips sparked a desire in me I had thought was dead. But his words of girls and auditions still rang in my ears. I like him but didn't know if the feeling is mutual.

We stop at the front door and Rich smiles at me. "I had a great time tonight."

"Me, too," I reply honestly. "That club was amazing."

"Can I call you again?"

"Yes," I reply, feeling as if every nerve in my body is wide awake waiting for him to touch me.

As if sensing this, Rich leans down and kisses me. I hesitate for only a moment before I kiss him back. I think back to his hands on me at the club, running down my hips and along my ass and I kiss him hard. He presses me against the door and kisses me hungrily. Then he pulls away from me, smiling.

"Goodnight," he says with a twinkle in his eye.

I watch him leave, feeling slightly confused. I'm so attracted to him. It feels as if he has a ton of secrets that I wish he would tell me. His hands on the dance floor had felt so good. Maybe I just need to get laid. But he's already driven away. Maybe he really isn't the bad boy I thought he was.

I suddenly need to catch my breath. I realize that maybe part of me wanted him to take things further.

Chapter Seven

A couple of days after my date with Rich, I head up to see Jon, who had called earlier and told me he had some news for me. I haven't heard from Rich yet, which makes me a little nervous. I had a nice time with him. Did he not feel the same? Maybe I am so blinded by my attraction to him that I didn't notice he had been bored.

My audition tape had been yesterday, and Jon had not been there. I couldn't help but be disappointed. He had only organized the meeting. The taping went okay. The director had me do a couple of readings and filmed it. At the end, he told me that I had a "natural love affair" with the camera, which I took as better than hearing I treat the camera like an ex-boyfriend.

I smooth out my hair in the rearview mirror. Kathy has let me take her car to see Jon. She asked me for non-stop details about Rich when she saw me but seemed to drop all conversation whenever I had brought up Jon. I am still convinced that something strange is going on.

I tell myself there is no need to be worried about seeing Jon. I clearly am not into him anymore, since I had such a great time with Rich. That is what I keep telling myself, anyway, as I walk down the hallway behind his assistant to his office.

Jon looks up from his computer. He is typing away, wearing glasses. My chest tightens. He looks amazing. I shake my head and step inside.

He looks up and smiles. "Jenny. Great, you're here."

"Hey, how are you?"

"Busy. But what else is new? Sorry I couldn't have been there yesterday, but I had a big event going on with one of my other clients."

I sit down. "No problem."

"Well, the director really loved you. Said you were a natural in front of the camera."

"That's good. Glad I have some sort of natural talent or else I'd have to be a waitress and tell everyone I really am an actor."

Jon laughs, and his eyes crinkle in an adorable way. "Well, I have some great news. I sent your video off to some different casting agents. One of them wants you to come in and do a reading."

"You're kidding!" I blurt out.

"Nope! I told you you're impressive, Jenny." His eyes stayed on me a beat too long and then he cleared his throat. "It's for a soap opera."

I try to recall the last time I had even watched a soap opera but nothing comes to mind. Don't they always have over-the-top plots with evil twin sisters or something?

I shrug. "Not a problem. I'll take what I can get."

"This is a big audition. I have to admit that I didn't think they'd call you in, due to your inexperience."

I think of Rich. Is he behind this? I want to ask but am afraid Jon will know instantly what I mean.

"Anyway," he goes on, "The audition is this Friday at two. You should make sure to bring your head shots and everything."

"You're not coming with me?"

Jon blinks. "That isn't the process normally."

"Oh." I say, disappointed.

"Are you okay?"

"I'm fine. I … I know sounds stupid, but I just didn't want to go alone."

Jon gets up from his desk and walks over to me, pulling a chair closer to mine and sitting back down. "Hey, don't worry about it. You'll be great. I can spot talent when I see it."

I smile a little back at him, aware at how close we are together. When he looks at me like this, he really does make me feel as if I can nail the audition.

"I didn't know you wore glasses," I say, pointing to his frames.

His hand goes to his face, and he looks embarrassed. "Oh, I didn't even realize I had them on. I usually wear contacts."

"They look good on you," I say without thinking.

Jon pauses for a moment and then smiles. "Sounds silly, but as a kid I was picked on for my glasses. So I stopped wearing them. I used to go to school and couldn't make out anything that was on the board. Stupid, right?"

"No, not stupid. I think everyone at that age really cared what kids in the class thought. I was bullied once for bringing this Barbie doll to school."

He frowns. "Wasn't that normal for little kids to do?"

I cringe. "It was actually in the eighth grade. I was completely mocked."

He laughs. "Well, I wouldn't have mocked you. Mostly because I wouldn't have been able to see you or your Barbie."

We laugh together this time, and I relax. He is easy to talk to. I'm glad I don't have some weird stuck up agent.

"So, what happened with your glasses?"

Jon leans back in his chair. "They sent a note home to my mom about my grades. I admitted the glasses story. She was so pissed. I told her about being teased but ultimately being grounded from video games was scarier. So I just dealt with it. Eventually the guys lost interest."

"How stupid. They're just glasses. Not exactly amazing bullying material."

"Are you saying your Barbie was?"

I wrinkle my nose. "My Barbie was flawless. They just didn't realize it."

A comfortable silence fills the room. I feel warm all over. I know there is absolutely no way that I should even read into my feelings for Jon. He is my agent. I'd had a fun date with Rich. But the ease of us swapping bullying stories and how confident Jon has sounded when he says I'd nail the audition makes my throat tighten.

"Who is the casting director on the soap?" I ask, trying to make my tone light.

But I can tell instantly that Jon knows what I am asking. "Not Rich. Why?"

"I was just curious," I lie, trying to back away from the subject. The last thing I want is for Jon to ask me about my date with him.

Jon looks at me closely. "Jenny, I'm your agent so I can't tell you how to live your life. But Rich is bad news."

"Why? Didn't you guys work together?"

"Yes. That's how I know he's bad news." He looks as if he wants to say more but cuts himself off.

"I'm being careful."

Jon nods and stands up, signaling the end of our personal conversation. "Remember, Friday is the audition. I'll text you with the details."

When I get home, Kathy is in the living room, painting her toe nails. She stands up when she sees me. She had looked exhausted this morning, having filmed some infomercial during the night, but now she looks excited.

"Guess what!"

"What?" I ask, pushing thoughts of Jon out of my head.

"I got an audition!"

"That's great! What's it for?"

"A soap opera," Kathy replies, and my heart drops. "Apparently for an actual role. I won't be Woman Drinking at Bar #4 this time."

My throat dries up. How do I tell her that I got the audition, too? It seems wrong, in a way, to be up for a part against Kathy. She is the entire reason that I am here, after all.

"Hey, why do you look like you just ate bad fish?"

"Nothing… nothing… it's just that… I'm up for that role, too."

To her credit, she only looks surprised for a moment before she smiles. "Really? Wow, that's great! I told you that Jon was a great agent. Plus with Rich working in casting that probably helped, too."

"Rich is in casting?" I echo as Kathy sits back down on the couch, her enthusiasm clearly dimmed.

"Oh yeah. He probably saw your audition tape."

"Jon said he wasn't part of casting."

"Oh, he's new to the soap. Started right before I sent my tape in."

"I'm sorry."

She looks up at me. "For what?"

"For getting this audition. Probably because I had a date with Rich. You deserve the part. I should call Jon and tell him that I won't do it."

But Kathy is already shaking her head. "No way, Jenny. Listen, I told you myself – Hollywood is all about who you know. Even if Rich got you this audition, you told me yourself that people think you have natural talent. So use it."

"But you deserve the part over me."

"All of us have equal shots at making this part. Apparently this soap opera wants fresh, new faces. It is all fair game to everyone auditioning."

I want to agree with her but I can't stop thinking about Rich. What if he gives me the part just because I went out on a date with him? I shouldn't have let him kiss me good-night. But being around him is so entrancing. He's dark and seductive and everything I like in a guy. Even now, just thinking about him, makes my skin warm.

I decide I will call him myself and see if he had any part in getting me the audition.

Chapter Eight

"I'm glad you wanted to see me again," Rich says with a smile.

"Thanks for picking me up," I reply, taking a sip of my iced coffee.

Rich ended up wanting to see me instead of talking on the phone. I had to admit it – I had wanted to see him again, too. Especially after the conversation in the office with Jon. I keep going back to it. The natural flow of our conversation. How easy sharing stories of our lame childhoods had gone. How handsome he looks.

Bad Jenny. Jon is my agent. To have feelings for him in any other regard is unprofessional. Anything I may have thought he feels about me is imagined. Agreeing to see Rich is dangerous, too, since I am paranoid about getting a part through dating him casually. But I decide it is less dangerous than actually thinking about Jon.

"Not a problem," Rich replies. "I'm thrilled to see you again. I'm sorry I didn't call you. I have been so busy with work since our date."

"I understand. Listen, I actually have a question. It probably sounds stupid since I'm new to all of this but I just have to know."

He waits. He is wearing a white button-up dress shirt today and black dress pants. I can tell he must work out on a regular basis. I catch myself wondering if he has a six pack underneath his clothes. I hope I'm not blushing.

"I got an audition for some soap opera," I rush on. "And so did my roommate. I was just making sure… I heard that… well, that Hollywood is all about who you know and…"

"Are you asking me if I'm the reason you got the audition?"

"Yes."

Rich laughs loudly, and a few people look over. "I am enchanted by how naïve you are to this business."

"Thanks. I think?"

"It's a compliment. Trust me." He reaches for my hand and holds it tightly. "You're different from most people in this town. I like that."

"That's great. Thanks." I am trying to say what I want to say perfectly. "But the audition…"

"Yes, I put in the good word when we got your tape."

I blanch, thinking of Kathy. She got the audition off of pure talent. I *have* gotten the audition because I had gone on a date with Rich.

Rich studies my face. "Why? Is that a problem? Normally people are very pleased when a connection gets them an audition."

"Right. I mean, I'm new to this. It just seems… wrong? I guess?" Under his gaze, I am stumbling over myself, suddenly unsure.

"Wrong? Honey, Hollywood is based all off of who you know. Surely someone has told you that before?"

He is right, someone has. Kathy. Her words echo in my brain. Maybe there truly is nothing to feel bad about, after all. Rich has gotten me the audition but it isn't as if he had gotten me the job. That will have to come from my pure talent. I probably won't get it, because I am so inexperienced.

"Yes, but my roommate is up for the part, too. And she said basically what you said – it's all about who you know."

"See? So no problem then." Rich smiles, taking a sip of his coffee.

"Right. No problem then."

Then why do I have such a strange feeling in my stomach?

<<<>>>

Friday comes quicker than I expected. At night, I can hear Kathy reciting her lines in her room. I try to go over my own lines, but feel self-conscious. Kathy sounds so great in her room. Any time I speak out loud, I sound completely out of my element. I am the definition of cold feet.

As I get ready in the bathroom Friday morning, my phone goes off. To my relief, it is Jon. I want to word vomit up all my insecurities to someone and doing it to Kathy seems wrong, given that we are both going after the same audition.

"I'm so glad you called," I say by way of greeting.

"Hello to you, too, Jenny." I can hear the amusement in his voice.

"I am seriously freaking out. This is my first audition, and I feel 110 percent confident that I am going to blow it."

"You were fabulous in the tapes we sent out, Jenny. You have a raw talent. You just have to know how to get it to shine. Maybe I should look into some acting lessons for you."

"That's great, except that won't help me *now*. I thought you'd be like 'Jenny, you're great, don't sweat it,' but instead you're bringing up acting lessons. Does this confirm I am completely out of my element here?"

"I have faith in you," Jon replies, dodging the question. "You can do it. I just called to wish you good luck."

"I wish you would be there," I blurt out as I try to find a piece of jewelry that would look best.

There is a moment of silence and I wonder if I have gone too far when Jon replies, "Me, too. I'm sorry but I have meetings with clients all afternoon. Why don't you meet me for coffee this evening? Unless you don't drink coffee past six?"

"No, I do. I drink coffee whenever. All the time." *You're rambling, shut up.* "But that sounds good."

"I'll text you later. Good luck, Jenny."

After he hangs up, I find myself staring at the phone. *Just an agent meeting*, I tell myself sternly, *nothing more to it than that.*

"I didn't realize so many people would be here," I whisper to Kathy as we sit down in chairs in a corner of the waiting room.

"It's usually like this the first go around. It won't thin out until they do callbacks."

I look around the room. Fifty other women of all sizes, shapes and colors are waiting to audition. When they say they are looking for new talent, they apparently aren't kidding. They aren't just looking for the tall blonde Hollywood type. I relax slightly. I am not such a sore thumb after all.

The girl next to me looks on the verge of tears as she mumbles through her lines. Across from us is another woman who looks as if she has been up for a week straight. Her movements are jerky. But for every strange sight I see, there are tons of other women who looked polished and ready to go. Kathy is one of them. I probably look like a scared kid on her first day at a new school.

"You'll be fine," Kathy whispers to me. "Honestly. Just be yourself and give it your all."

"Everyone else looks so experienced. I know Rich was doing me a favor but maybe he shouldn't have."

"Don't be silly. Seriously, Jenny, you moved out here for this. Take this chance."

I look at Kathy closely. Anything sour she may have felt over me getting this audition is gone. Either she is a great actress or she truly is okay with it. In order to save my sanity, I decide to think of it as her being okay with it.

"I still think I'm going to blow it. Jon called while I was getting ready and didn't come right out to say it, but I can tell he isn't expecting me to get a callback either." I sigh. "I guess I can tell him how it goes when we meet for coffee."

"You're meeting with Jon for coffee?"

"Yeah, once he is done with his meetings for the day."

"How nice of him," Kathy replies, her tone curt.

I find myself studying her face. It is subtle but her features have definitely tightened. *I knew I wasn't imagining it.*

"Yeah," I reply slowly, wanting to change the subject. "Anyway, I'm sure I won't have much to say."

"Jon is very involved with his clients," Kathy says and then she looks at me, forcing a smile on her face. "He'll give you tips, I'm sure."

I open my mouth to reply when a name is called. The first woman, a perfectly polished redhead, goes in to the room, shutting the door behind her. I exhale and push thoughts of Kathy and Jon out of my head. Time to review my lines.

Kathy goes in before me. She texts me twenty minutes later to tell me she is waiting for me downstairs in the lobby. All I can do now is wait. I watch the other girls go in and not return. The girl next to me looks as though she might burst into tears when her name is called. *I wonder what her story is,* I think as I watch her go.

By the time my name is called, there are about ten of us left. My feet feel like lead as I make my way into the room. There are three people in the room.

A tall balding man in the middle waves at me. "Jenny, right?"

"Yes, sir," I reply meekly.

"I'm August Grant. I'm the producer. This is my assistant, Amanda Fields and the head casting director, Billy Arch."

A thin blonde woman smiles at me. Next to her, a gruff-looking man, obviously Billy, nods his head.

"It's nice to meet you." I try not to let the camera filming the audition make me nervous.

"Now, if you'd like to step to the middle of the room. We're going to start with the first scene, okay?"

I take a deep breath.

I press the elevator button, trying to control the sinking feeling in my gut. Part of me wants to cry. The other part of me just feels like an idiot. Why had I thought I could do this? I feel confident I have messed up the audition. The logical part of me is saying I didn't come off it as badly as I think I did. But the louder, nagging voice in my brain says I was terrible.

The first scene went okay. I ended up downplaying almost everything so it fell a little flat. I could tell Mr. Grant and his assistant were perplexed. But it was Billy Arch who was brutally honest with me.

"That was dull," he says, furrowing his thick eyebrows. "In this scene, your step-sister is in a coma and your boyfriend is accusing you of being the reason she almost died. We need to feel that from you – the horror that your boyfriend could accuse you of such a thing."

The next take is on the other end of the spectrum. Completely bonkers. But if my non-existent boyfriend had accused me of such a thing, of course I am going to completely flip out, right?

Wrong.

"Let's try it again," Billy says with a shake of his head. "But in the middle this time, Jenny. Less mentally unhinged, more aghast and horrified."

Trying not to act flustered, I go through the scene one more time. This time, Amanda writes something down on a sheet of paper and August nods at her.

"Okay, great. You've got a lot of energy," Billy says, looking at my head shot. "I can see that you're new to the rodeo. That's fine. We're looking for new talent. But you might want to figure out how to properly channel the energy you're feeling. You take any acting classes?"

"No, sir."

"You need to. Let's skip to scene three and run through it."

This scene was the overly dramatic one where my character decides that popping pills would solve all her problems. By this point, I am feeling so flustered, like I have fucked it all up, that I go through it without needing to glance at my paper once.

Yet their faces are blank when I finish. Billy ends the audition after that scene. There is no mention of a

callback. There is nothing to read off their faces. I feel
like a complete failure.

I try to tell myself it doesn't matter. There is no way
that I would have gotten the part. I wouldn't have even
gotten the audition if it hadn't been for Rich. I should
start small. Back to my dream of a tampon commercial,
I suppose. Oh well. Kathy deserves the part – more than
I do.

I try to repeat that mantra as I step onto the main
floor of the building we are in. I promptly stop. By the
front desk is Kathy… and Jon. He is holding flowers in
one hand. My heart skips a beat. Both of their faces are
drawn tight and it looks as if they are bickering. That
can't be correct. What could they possibly bicker
about?

I steel myself and walk over. As soon as they see
me, they both try to hide the expressions on their faces.
I decide I will play dumb. I wave as I walk over,
making sure to look like I haven't noticed anything
peculiar.

"Hey," I say, smiling. "I thought you had meetings
with clients."

Jon looks sheepish. "I do. But I wanted to swing by
and see you. These are for you." He hands me the
bouquet of flowers.

My face flushes. I didn't think that they were meant
for me. I take the flowers gingerly.

"You didn't have to do that," I reply. "Really. I'm sure I bombed the audition."

"I'm sure you did fine," Kathy interjects.

I glance at her, trying to gauge her mood but her face is blank. "I don't know. When I left, they had no expression on their faces. I have no idea how they felt about my performance."

"It's your first audition. Don't be so hard on yourself," Kathy replies.

"How did it go with you?"

Kathy's gaze flicks to Jon. "Fine. Listen, I'll wait for you in the car, okay?"

I watch her leave, frowning. First, the two of them were bickering and now Kathy's sudden exit. I turn to look at Jon. "What was that about?"

"What?"

"I don't know," I lie. "She just seemed off, don't you think?"

"Did she? Anyway, I'm sure you did fine on the audition. I really wouldn't worry."

"Maybe," I reply, smelling the flowers. "You really didn't have to get me these though."

"Just think of it as an apology for not being able to be here for the audition. And the fact that something came up so I can't have coffee with you tonight."

I want to hide behind the flowers. I am pretty sure I am blushing. There is no way that agents usually bought their clients flowers, right? I wasn't sure. It seems like it wouldn't be the case. But it isn't as if I have a ton to go off of. I didn't want to read too much into something that isn't really there. Do I really deserve flowers because he had something come up?

"Well, they are beautiful. Thanks."

"No problem. I have to head out because I have another meeting, but I'm glad that I was able to catch you."

"Me, too."

"I'll call you once I hear something."

I nod and watch him leave. My heart beating loudly in my chest. I cling to the flowers, watching him depart. Coming all this way to see how I did. Giving me these flowers. Is it crazy that maybe he has a crush on me, or is it merely wishful thinking?

Chapter Nine

On the way home, Kathy makes small talk about the audition but doesn't mention Jon or the flowers. She is acting okay with me. If she is really mad at me for having Jon as my agent, wouldn't she say something?

In any case, when we get home, Kathy goes to her room, claiming she is going to have a nap. I decide to put the flowers in my room. When my phone goes off, I realize it is Rich.

"What are you doing tonight?" he asks when I pick up.

"Well, I had plans but they fell through."

"Come out with me."

"And do what?"

"What do you want to do? Clubbing? Dinner?"

"Honestly, I'm pretty tired. How about just a movie?"

We agree on a time for him to pick me up. I decide to let Kathy know that I am going to be leaving. When I come out, she is already in the living room with an overnight bag.

"Hey, what's going on?"

"My friend is having a birthday party in West Hollywood. I figured I'll probably be too drunk to drive so I'm just going to crash there. You okay for the night?"

I nod. "I'm seeing Rich tonight anyway."

Kathy's shoulders relax slightly. "Okay. Well, be safe."

"So, anything you wanted to see?" Rich asks as we pull up into the movie theater parking lot.

"I probably should have picked one out beforehand. Nothing sad, I know that."

"Okay. We'll just see what's playing."

Rich looks amazing tonight. His sandy blond hair falls in his eyes a little and he is wearing a black button-up shirt and dress pants. I keep thinking back to us on the dance floor from our last date. I want his hands on me. I can feel the energy vibrating between the two of us. He wants me, too.

"How did the audition go?" he asks casually.

I shrug. "Okay, I think. Hard to tell by their lack of facial expressions so I guess we'll just have to wait and see."

"I'm sure you did fine. They always keep blank faces. Treat it all so seriously."

"Why weren't you sitting in on the auditions?"

"I'm not the head casting director. I only have some say in what goes on there."

I think about Jon saying he is bad news. I wish I knew what had happened between the two of them.

"It's fine. My friend Kathy is up for the same spot. She deserves it."

"Whoa," he replies, grabbing my hand. "Don't say that. She doesn't deserve it any more than you do."

"I don't know. She's been in this business a lot longer than I have."

"But she isn't one of my girls. You are. You deserve it just as much as she does." He lets go of my hand. "Now, let's go see a movie."

As we walk up to the theater, I find myself turning his words over in my head. This isn't the first time he has mentioned his "girls". There is no way I should expect us to be exclusive – even I don't want to be thinking about that yet. But being lumped in with whoever else he is seeing, as if we are all part of his harem, rubs me the wrong way.

"Girls?" I say suddenly, stopping in my tracks.

Rich stops and looks at me. "What?"

"You said I'm one of your… girls. What does that mean exactly? How many women are you seeing?"

"Why?" He moves out of the way of people walking up to the theater and leans against the side of the building. "Do you want to be exclusive?"

"What?" I blurt out, feeling suddenly as if my words have come out all wrong. "No. No offense but we just started dating."

"Then why is it a problem if I see other women?"

"I guess just how you word it. Like we're all in some gang where you are our leader or something."

Rich leans close to me. I can faintly smell cigarette smoke on his breath. He trails his fingertips down my arms, which causes goose bumps to pop up along my body. I shiver in spite of myself.

"I'm sorry I made you feel that way. I won't say it again," he whispers, his eyes bright and yet somehow stormy at the same time. "Is that okay?"

"Yes, that's fine," I mumble as he wraps his arms around me and pulls me in for a kiss.

The kiss starts a heat deep inside of me. I can feel it start in my chest and then slowly roll out along the rest of my body as I push myself against him and kiss him back hard. Any time he touches me, all the thoughts in my brain simply fall out of my head.

Rich pulls away first. My chest is rising and falling quickly, and I try to steady myself. He smiles at me – a dark smile with a promise of things to come.

"Let's go into the movie now," he mumbles in my ear.

During the entire movie, I overthink everything on top of fighting my growing desire to throw myself at Rich. My body just melts when he touches me – it's been ages since I felt like that about anyone. I really want to sleep with him.

On the other hand, I am also attracted to Jon, even though I try to deny it. But I have no idea how Jon feels about me. I am terrified about reaching out for him. What if I am just misunderstanding the attention and our seeming connection to one another and end up rejected? After Paul and Robbs, I can't handle any rejection. It will cut me to my core. Can I risk ruining a professional relationship all because I think *maybe* Jon likes me, too?

But Rich is a sure thing. He feels strongly for me. There are no worries about rejection with him. He wants me, and I want him. I glance over at him in the darkness of the theater, my heart pounding in my chest. He is watching the movie, a somewhat bored expression on his face. He looks over at me and smiles. My heart constricts.

<<◇>>

Rich drives me home in mostly silence. When he pulls up in my apartment complex, I look at him.

"My roommate is gone for the night. Would you like to come up?"

"I would love that," he replies.

We stumble into the apartment, our arms thrown around each other, kissing each other for dear life. The heat between us makes my heart race so fast that in any other situation I would have to lay down. Instead, I press myself harder against him. We are in the living room. He reaches for my shirt, and I suddenly get nervous and move away.

"Give me one second," I whisper, hoping I sound sexy as I turn to go into the bathroom.

Once in the bathroom, I take a deep breath. My skin is flushed and my face is red. I am burning up with desire. It is moving quickly, so I need a second to breathe. I am nervous about sleeping with someone again. I splash some water on my face and go back out into the living room.

"Sorry about that."

Rich is sitting on the couch and pats the spot next to him. I sit down and exhale. He leans over and kisses me gently along my neck. I catch my breath and my skin is tingling. Rich kisses down my neck and then gently tilts my face to his. His eyes are full of fire, like a blue storm, when he kisses me hard on the mouth.

I melt into him. All concerns about being nervous vanish away as I slip my tongue in his mouth and kiss him back. His hands are on my legs, inching up my skirt.

"You're so hot," he whispers in my ear as he kisses my neck. "So fucking sexy."

In reply, I start to unbutton his shirt. When it finally slips off, I see that I have been right about his six pack. My heart thuds as he removes my own shirt. The air in the apartment is cool to my skin. I am suddenly glad that I wore my nice black bra tonight. It pushes my breasts up to make nice cleavage.

Rich likes what he sees and begins to kiss my breasts. I moan softly, closing my eyes. I feel him unclasp my bra and then fondle my breasts, gently taking each nipple in his mouth and sucking on it. He gently pushes me back on the couch and moves my skirt up around my waist. Rich stands above me as he takes off his pants. I watch, wanting nothing more than for him to be inside of me as soon as he can.

He slides down his pants and his stiff manhood strains against his boxers. Rich pulls them off as well, stroking himself in front of me.

"Do you like this?" he asks.

"Yes," I breathe, "I like it."

"I'm going to fuck you," Rich says gruffly.

The words give me a thrill, and I nod as he slides over me. When our skin touches, I sigh in delight. He is giving off so much body heat. He nudges open my thighs and enters me.

I moan, closing my eyes as I take him inside of me. Rich bites and licks my nipples as he begins to thrust inside of me. He feels so good that I begin to moan louder, wrapping my legs around him in an effort to try to get him deeper inside of me. There is nothing else in my mind besides Rich fucking me. I rock my hips as I take him inside of me.

Rich thrusts hard and fast in me, moving one hand down to my clit. He moves his finger expertly over it, bringing my moans harder and stronger. I am sure the people in the apartments next to us can hear me but I don't care. The sensations of Rich inside of me as well as moving his finger along my clit is too much to take. I climax.

I cry out his name and shake against him as my orgasm rocks through me. It is so intense that I am panting. Rich is whispering my name in my ear, telling me how sexy I look as I climax.

When my climax subsides, he increases his thrusts. Rich rocks hard and fast inside of me. He looks so good as he fucks me. I cling to him until he grunts my name and pounds hard inside of me. His climax shudders through him as he comes hard.

When he finishes, he rests his head on my chest. We both are soaked in sweat, panting heavily with our limbs entwined. Slowly, Rich detangles himself from me.

"Where is your room?" he whispers. "Let's go to bed."

I lead him to my room.

Chapter Ten

I wake up the next morning from a terrible dream where I am falling down the stairs. Every time I hit the bottom, I am suddenly back at the top of the staircase with Robbs bearing down on me.

My skin is cold and clammy when I wake up. My heart races in my chest, spurned on from the fear of falling. The sunlight that comes in from my room gives me some comfort. If the room was pitch black, I would be panicking more.

Instead, I turn to my right. . I'm in my bed alone. For a second, I think maybe I have imagined the entire night with Rich. After we had sex on the couch, we stumbled to the bedroom, where he woke me up once in the middle of the night to have sex again. But there is a sheet of paper on the pillow, folded over, which lets me know it wasn't a dream after all.

I snatch the paper up and open it up to read:

I had a great time last night. I had a meeting this morning and couldn't bear to wake you up from your sleep.

Call you later,

Rich

I feel mildly disappointed that Rich hadn't woken me up to say goodbye. I lay back down, mulling over my thoughts. Sleeping with Rich was passionate and exciting. I enjoyed the time we spent together.

So why am I thinking about Jon?

Frustrated, I get up and grab clean clothes to take a shower. I make sure to get my clothes from the living room as well, so I don't have to deal with Kathy asking questions. Plus, she probably wouldn't want someone screwing on her couch.

I feel better after the shower. When I get out, I see that I have a voicemail on my phone from Jon. My grip on my phone tightens. I look at the flowers in my room and listen to the voicemail.

"Hey, Jenny. Call me back ASAP, okay?"

I wish he had left more details. I call back instantly, nervous about what he is going to say.

He answers on the second ring and sounds out of breath. "Hey! I'm so glad you called back!"

"What's up?" I try to sound casual.

"The casting director from the soap opera audition called me this morning."

My heart drops. I guess I'll be having my first official rejection today.

"You got a callback! This Monday!"

"What?" I stammer, certain I heard him wrong.

"You got a callback, Jenny. They liked how well you took direction. They want you to come back for the second round."

"Oh my god! I can't believe it!"

"I knew you'd do well! I told you!"

"Thank you, Jon. I can't believe it. I thought for sure that would never happen. I mean, just a callback is a reason to celebrate for me."

"It's amazing for your first audition, but you have the talent to pull through. You should celebrate."

I bite my tongue and then decide to go for it. "Why don't you celebrate with me? We could grab drinks somewhere."

Long pause. I suddenly feel like an idiot. I can try to pass this off as merely an agent/client meeting but something in the silence lets me know he knows I didn't mean it just as that.

Finally, Jon clears his throat. "That sounds great."

"Really?"

"Yeah. Are you free tonight around eight?"

We make plans to meet up at a place around the corner, so I don't have to borrow Kathy's car. Plus, I can make it sound as if it is just a quick meeting in case she asks anything. That is when I hear the front door shut. I walk out to say hi to her and see her beaming at me.

"I got a callback for the soap opera!" Kathy trills, looking excited.

"I did, too!" I manage to muster up some enthusiasm to match her good news.

I tense up, waiting for her to look irritated at me but all she does is look excited. She comes over and hugs me.

"Isn't this exciting?" she asks. "I hope it goes well for us."

I do, too. But there is a possibility of it only going well for one of us.

"Did you really think that was going to work?"

Jon laughs and shakes his head. "No, but I had no clue what I was doing."

I laugh and pop a chip into my mouth. It is a little after eight. Jon and I have settled down at a Mexican restaurant around the corner from my apartment. I am hoping that the conversation with Jon will wash away the one I had just had with Kathy.

She asked where I was going. Sensing that I should probably lie but not quite sure why I feel that way, I opted to tell her that I am going to see Jon to celebrate the callback.

Kathy stiffens and a dark cloud passes over her face.

"How nice of him to offer," she repeats, an earlier echo of the flower exchange.

"It was me," I say, trying to protect Jon from… I am not even sure what exactly. "I offered, since he helped me so much."

"Just be careful, Jenny. Don't get in over your head."

"What does that mean?"

But Kathy evades my question and heads to her room. The entire exchange has left a bad taste in my mouth. Obviously something besides a family emergency was the reason that Kathy has left Jon as her agent. But why recommend him to me?

"You okay?"

I snap out of my thoughts. Jon comes back into focus. He is wearing his glasses tonight, with a loose-fitting dress shirt and dress pants. His hair is a bit messy, but naturally messy, unlike when Rich tries to style it that way. His smile is easy going, and I feel relaxed just looking at it.

"Yeah, sorry… just… thinking about the callback," I lie, not wanting to ruin the moment by bringing up Kathy.

"You'll be great. I wouldn't worry about it. Even if you don't get the part, consider this experience under your belt."

"You're right. I know I should. I just don't want to fuck it up when I get in there."

"You won't. It'll be the same group as the last time, although Rich might be there," he says with a slight scowl.

"Rich?"

"Yeah, he had a hand in the selection for the callbacks."

"You mean I have to act in front of *Rich*?"

"Yes, why?" Something dawns on his face. "Did you really… I mean, are you seeing him, officially? I know I heard you guys mention a date before but…"

"We've seen each a couple of times," I reply, hoping I don't blush when I think about how we slept together. "But we aren't officially together or anything."

Jon shifts in his chair. "I know it isn't my business, but Rich is bad news."

"You've said that before, but haven't exactly given me anything specific," I point out.

The waitress comes by at this point and we order our food. When she departs, Jon runs his fingers through his hair.

"Rich and I used to work together. We opened my office together, actually. But I wasn't a fan of how he did business. He was shady. He used to openly hit on all our clients, even if they were married or seeing someone. I suspected him of sleeping with all the women and making promises to them of getting roles if they did so. So we fought, and he left the business. Went on to be a casting agent."

"Sleeping with women and giving them roles?" I ask for clarification, my brain buzzing.

"He's got that over-confidence a lot of women like. I get it, whatever. If that is your thing, it's cool. But Rich is more than a player. He's a sleaze. He's bad news. I never proved anything he did but I just don't trust him."

A cold feeling goes through my stomach. The chips and salsa suddenly taste bland in my mouth.

"I have to use the restroom, excuse me," I mumble and head toward the ladies' room.

Fortunately the restroom is empty – I lean against the sink and try to clear my head. I didn't sleep with Rich just so that he would give me something in return. I would have never thought to discuss such a thing. There was no mention of offers or exchanges. I had gotten that first audition due to connections, not because I was dating Rich.

I tell myself I am being silly. Jon has never proven Rich was sleeping with these women in exchange for roles. I just need to calm down. Enjoy whatever is happening between Jon and me. Think twice about seeing Rich again.

The rest of dinner flies by in record time. Jon thrills me with tales of his childhood and makes me laugh so hard my sides hurt. I find myself enchanted with the colorful way he tells stories and how easily it is to be attracted to him. By the time we leave the restaurant, I have butterflies in my stomach that I have never felt around Rich.

"Let me walk you home," Jon says, once we step outside. "It's just around the corner, right?"

I nod and we set off. Part of me wishes he would hold my hand. Another part of me is saying that I am falling hard for him and should back away.

"So, I never asked you what brought you to Hollywood. That's a big change to make."

Memories flash in my head, all of them bad. I fall silent for a moment, unsure of how to answer.

Jon speaks up again, "Did I say something wrong? You have a funny look on your face."

"No, no, I'm fine. Nothing good brought me to Hollywood. I just needed to get away from where I was."

"Bad memories?"

"You could say that," I reply. "I… I was pregnant… and then lost the baby."

I can't believe I said that. My mouth went dry as soon as the words left me. Saying it out loud brings back the nightmare of falling down the stairs, with Robbs' hands on my back, pushing me down.

"Wow, Jenny. That's horrible. I'm sorry. I don't even know what to say."

"It's okay. I'm sorry. You probably wanted some funny story and here I am blabbing out some nonsense."

"No," Jon replies firmly. "It isn't nonsense. I'm sorry that happened to you."

I don't feel like telling the rest of the story of how I lost my child so I just nod. We walk in silence. Jon looks as if he wants to hold my hand but at the last second he changes his mind and slips his hand into his pocket. I sink into my thoughts. Are we into each other or is he just seeing this as a client/agent meeting? The signs are so confusing.

We get to my apartment, and I unlock the front door. "Wait here, I'll get the money."

I had foolishly forgotten my wallet when I left to see him. I feel bad making Jon foot the entire bill and want to at least give him some cash so we are even. I dart into my bedroom for my wallet, grab some money and head back to the front door when I hear Kathy talking to Jon. I flatten myself against the wall in the kitchen, straining to hear.

"… tell her about us…" Kathy says, sounding irritated.

"There isn't anything going on with Jenny and me," Jon replies and my heart drops.

"Does she know that, Jon?" She is whispering, which makes it harder to hear. "Do you know that?"

"Of course…"

"Does she… that we used to be together?"

Wait, what?

"No," Jon replies.

"Are you going to… that we used to date?"

My heart thuds in my chest. They used to *date*? Everything snaps into place. How strange the two of them act around each other. How Kathy got so irritated when Jon brought me flowers. I suddenly feel stupid. Not only is Jon saying that he has no feelings for me but he dated Kathy. I am so stupid.

Turning on my heels, I go into the living room and shove the money at Jon. "Here you go. You can leave now."

Jon blanches. "Jenny, wait."

"Please leave," I say stiffly and close the door in his face.

I turn around and Kathy is fiddling with the buttons on her shirt. "Listen, Jenny. I didn't mean for you to overhear that."

"Well, I did!" I snap.

"I wanted to tell you the truth. That Jon and I had dated. I really did. But I didn't know a right time for it."

"Seriously? You couldn't find a right time in any of the times we were talking? Or when Jon was coming around? Or when you told me to call Jon to represent me? Why would you even do that, by the way? If you two used to date, why do something that would bother you?"

"Because it didn't bother me until Jon started hanging out with you," she admits, averting her eyes. "He shouldn't… he shouldn't go after clients. It's how we started dating and it just rubbed salt in the wound. I haven't seen anyone since… since we broke up." Kathy is stammering over her words now, looking upset. "So when he started flirting with you, it just pissed me off."

"So you're upset he was moving on?"

"No. Yes. I just didn't like him going after you. Where I would have to see it, Jenny. It has nothing to do with you."

"You heard what he said. He said he had no feelings for me in that way. So all of this is just him being friendly."

Kathy shakes her head. "No way. He's just trying to save my feelings. Listen, I know you're upset I wasn't honest with you. I get it. But it really isn't that big of a deal, Jenny, really."

The fact she is now trying to dictate my feelings is pissing me off. She has no idea how I feel. Trying to tell me that it is okay and not a big deal is simply invalidating my own emotions. It rubs me the wrong way, and I can feel myself closing up. I feel stupid. Knowing that Jon and Kathy had a history makes me feel as if I am just being used to make her jealous or something. Jon had declared that he didn't have feelings for me. I have misread everything and now look like a jackass. Is he trying to make Kathy jealous?

If he is, it seems to be working. She can tell me that it is because she doesn't want me to go through what she has gone through, but I don't fully believe it. Kathy doesn't like seeing Jon flirt with me. I am stuck in the middle of their mind games.

"Jon is a really good agent," Kathy goes on, not noticing my darkening mood. "I truly thought he would help you. And he has! It has nothing to do with you seeing him as an agent. I just don't think you two should see each other—"

"I don't care what you want," I snap, storming back to my room to get an overnight bag. "I don't appreciate getting pulled in the middle of your mind games with Jon."

"Jenny!"

I start shoving some things in my bag, wondering where I can go. I need to cool down. It isn't as if I know a lot of people in this city. The only person left for me is Rich. My reservations about him fly out the window. Jon probably lied about him at dinner as well.

I call Rich and wait for him to pick up. "Can I see you?"

Chapter Eleven

Rich drives me to a place I have only seen in movies and TV shows.

"You live in *Beverly Hills*?" I say, my face practically planted against the window of his car.

Rich chuckles. "It isn't a big deal."

"Are you kidding me? Of course it is. I bet my apartment fits into your closet."

Rich turns into a gated community, swiping a code that opens up the ornate gate. As we drive into the community, all thoughts of what has been stressing me out fly from my mind. The homes – make that mansions – are massive. I can't believe that people can actually afford something like this. We drive past them slowly with Rich obviously letting me take in the expansiveness of these enormous urban palaces.

"Mine isn't as big as some of these," he says. "I wouldn't get too excited."

I wave my hand in his direction, my eyes still glued to the window. "Whatever. When people say Hollywood, this is what everyone truly means." I pause for a moment and then look at him. "How did you get so successful anyway?"

"Ah, if you're thinking it is all from my job, I'm going to disappoint you. I was born into money."

"Lucky," I grumble, looking back out the window.

We turn another corner. This street has smaller houses, although they are still massive in relation to anything I've seen back home. Rich turns his car into one of the driveways of a spacious, well-maintained, two-story house. *A far cry from the dollhouse,* I muse as I get out of the car. Clutching my overnight bag, I trail after Rich toward the front door.

He holds open the door for me and I step inside. We are in a large foyer with low lighting. There is a painting on one wall and marble flooring underneath my feet. I think back to Underwater Nosh and how overwhelmed I had felt when I had merely stepped into the coat room. I feel the same thing now.

"Want a tour?" he asks.

"Oh, definitely!"

He leads me through the house. I marvel at how large his kitchen is – he could easily fit twenty people in the kitchen alone. The dining room has an oak table and windows that overlook the pool. The living room is modern, with all sorts of tech-savvy stuff I probably can't figure out on my own. He leads me up the stairs to the second floor. He stops in the guest room, which looks exactly like something I would see in a five-star hotel.

"This is where you can sleep tonight," Rich says, although his tone is overly light, as if he is suggesting I don't have to if I don't want to.

"Okay," I reply, keeping things vague on purpose.

I am still fuming over what Kathy has said and how I feel used by Jon. And no matter what anyone has said about Rich, he hasn't done anything to hurt me. Maybe I am a fool. Jon is obviously a bad guy wrapped up in a nice guy exterior. No one wants to be used to make someone jealous, including me.

I trail into the bathroom and for the first time since I stormed out of the apartment, I check my phone. I had put it on silent, not wanting to deal with it. There are two calls from Kathy and three from Jon. Two voicemails. Two text messages. I shove my phone back in my purse. I'm not interested in hearing anything they have to say right now. Not while Kathy tries to tell me how to feel and being used by Jon.

"Lost in the bathroom?" Rich peeks his head in.

I turn around, flustered. "Yeah. I mean, a rain shower in the guest room? What do your parents do anyway?"

"They're heavily involved in the stock market," Rich replies, motioning me to follow him out of the guest room.

"Damn, I should have gotten involved in that, too."

Rich walks past a billiards room and opens a door at the end of the hall. I step inside and look around, mouth agape. His bedroom is luxurious, all dark browns and reds. There are floor-to-ceiling windows on one side that open out onto the patio – I notice a hot tub. A big screen TV is on the wall across from the bed. There's an ensuite bathroom, which is probably massive as well.

"This is incredible," I breathe as Rich moves behind me, placing his hands on my shoulders.

"A soak in the hot tub would probably help you unwind, you know," Rich whispers in my ear.

I close my eyes. I briefly mention to him that I had gotten into a fight with Kathy over the audition and need to cool down. The thought of melting into a hot tub sounds perfect.

"I don't have a suit," I reply, opening my eyes at the sudden thought.

Rich smiles against my skin. "Do we really need suits?"

That flame of desire sparks up inside of me again. Not caring about anything to do with Kathy and Jon, I turn around and head toward the guest room to slip out of my clothes.

I let out a sigh of delight. The bubbles feel amazing against my skin. I lean back and close my eyes. I have told Rich I wanted to get in the hot tub first. I am nervous about strolling out onto the patio naked. He agreed, and is waiting for me to get settled. It has been ages since I relaxed in a hot tub.

"Are you ready?" he asks.

"All set."

I keep my eyes closed. It sounds silly, but the thought of seeing Rich naked and getting in the hot tub makes me blush. All this luxury and money… I am feeling out of my league. He probably can have models or celebrities. What in the world does he see in me, some newbie who hasn't even had a single role yet?

"Feels good, doesn't it?"

I open my eyes. He is across from me, looking out at the view. I swear that I can see what could be considered comparable to a waterpark in one of the mansions a ways off.

"Fantastic," I say lazily, finally starting to forget what was bothering me earlier. "I would soak in this every night if I could."

"I have to admit that I don't use it enough."

"That's a shame," I mumble, closing my eyes again.

We both fall silent, enjoying the bubbles. I try not to think about Rich's body and the skilled way he had made me orgasm the last time we had slept together. It is difficult to find a man who knows how to treat you in bed. Rich is very good at that.

"What are you thinking about?" he asks suddenly.

I hope he can't see me blushing as I open my eyes to look at him. "Nothing. Kathy, I guess," I lie.

"She needs to get over it. It's show business."

"Right."

"She shouldn't feel threatened by you. If she had confidence in her skills, she wouldn't be so concerned you got a callback."

"Yeah. I know, you're right," I reply, wanting to switch the subject.

"It's 'cause she probably has all these stupid ideas of how Hollywood works from Jon," he scoffs.

Intrigued, I decide to pursue this topic. "You worked with Jon, right?"

Rich eyes me. "He didn't say anything about me?"

I shake my head, hoping my face is blank. I am interested in what Rich has to say about Jon.

"He has his head in the clouds. He came to Hollywood with nothing. I was the one who hired him. His code of ethics doesn't match what goes on in this business. His ideals are so pure that while he is a great agent for people like you, new to the industry, I really have to suggest you dump him once you get some real work under your belt. I can suggest some people for you."

"So you left the company because you two just didn't see eye to eye?"

"Jon didn't want to get his hands dirty. Unless, you know, it was with his own clients. Although I'm sure you know all about Kathy and Jon."

"Oh, yeah. She mentioned it ages ago," I lie, fuming that Rich knows this and I have been left in the dark.

"You shouldn't date your own clients. They had that messy break up, and he lost a rising star because of his stupidity."

"Kathy was pretty vague on why they broke up." I can't help myself, I want to know every stupid detail. "Do you know why?"

"Kathy said he wouldn't commit. Jon said he just wasn't ready to settle down yet. Anyway, he harps on me for what I do or what he *thinks* I do, but he isn't that swell of a guy either."

I try to match up Rich's dark words against what I know about Jon. I even told Jon about Maggie, something that still torments me when I think about it. Opening up like that is rare for me. I have kept everything inside of me locked up so tightly yet I shared something so personal with him without even knowing him for very long. What will he do with this information? How can I keep him as my agent when I have feelings for him?

It is stupid to even think about the feelings I have for him. I have feelings for Rich, too, I tell myself as I look at him. He is handsome and well off and has great connections. So why am I so upset about Jon and his history with Kathy? I should just forget about him completely. Rich can help me find another agent.

"Let's not talk about those idiots anymore," Rich says roughly, sliding across the hot tub toward me.

He tilts his head down and kisses me. He tastes faintly of the water in the hot tub. I kiss him back, sinking into him. His hands go around my waist, holding me tightly against the side of the hot tub. I wrap my arms around his neck. Rich is the guy for me. I don't need to torment myself over Jon any longer.

We stay like that for a while, making out in the hot tub. His kisses are hot and slowly growing hungrier. Our bare bodies press against each other. I can feel the bubbles on our skin. The sun has fully set now, leaving us only guided by the lights from the hot tub. The whole thing feels as if I am in some sort of fever dream. All I focus on is holding onto Rich and kissing him.

Finally he breaks apart from me. "Want to come inside?"

"Won't we get the bed wet?" I mumble, feeling dazed.

He laughs and I blush. "The last thing on my mind right now is good housekeeping," he grins at me. I realize how ridiculous that must have sounded considering the moment. We get out of the hot tub, and he leads me to his giant bed. We stop in front of it, and he looks me over, drinking me in with his eyes.

"You're so sexy," Rich whispers.

"So are you," I reply, kissing him.

He kisses me back, and I lower myself to my knees, taking him in my mouth. He lets out a groan as I move my tongue up and down his length slowly, teasing him. Rich is stiff and warm, throbbing. I move my head up and down as I suck on him, rolling my tongue around the tip of his cock. He shudders and moans my name.

I work on him like this for a little bit, enjoying the feel of him inside my mouth. Rich has a nice cock and I like sucking on the tip and then taking the rest of it in my mouth.

Finally he moves away from me. "I need to fuck you," he says gruffly.

I am out of breath and my head feels light. I want it, too. I get on the bed but he shakes his head.

"I want you to ride me. I want to watch you."

Emboldened by how sexy he thinks I am, I straddle him after he lays down. I sink slowly down on his cock, moaning a little as he fully fills me. Once I got settled, I began to ride him. Rich reaches his hands up to my breasts.

My clit rubs against him, sending shivers of delight through me. I arch my back and ride him harder, liking the tremors that work through me. Rich is moaning loudly, gripping my breasts and squeezing them. Whenever our skin touches, I can feel how warm we are. The moonlight casts a light on us, and I rock against him so hard I can hear the bed moving slightly.

The sensations of riding him and feeling him inside me send me over the edge. I let out a gasp and cry his name as I come, shuddering hard. Suddenly, Rich takes hold of my hips and starts to pound inside of me, fucking me so hard that it only makes me peak harder. He is hitting my G-spot, I realize, as he fucks me. I cling to him as I come again. My moans have turned into screams of passion as Rich comes as well. He moans loudly, his orgasm rocking through him as though his entire body is vibrating.

When we finish, I collapse on top of him. We are both covered in sweat. Sleep grabs a hold of me and pulls me in. I don't resist.

Chapter Twelve

I go back home the next day. As incredible as it was escaping for a night with Rich, there is no way I can avoid these problems forever. Being with Rich has clarified what I need to do. Whatever feelings I have for Jon are not going to be reciprocated. I would be stupid to focus on what I have felt for him. He obviously isn't the type of person I thought he was.

As for Kathy, she still has given me a lot of help to get out of the spot where I had been depressed and lost. I am not pleased with the situation, but for the sake of us living together, I need to forgive her. I have to be the bigger person.

I also figure Kathy will give me another agent to call and see if I can switch agencies. I don't want to ask Rich for a favor like that yet, especially since he will ask why I want to switch. The last thing I feel like explaining to Rich is how I thought Jon and I could be something.

I walk in the front door of our apartment to see Kathy reading a book in the living room. I have readied myself for a conversation with her.

When she sees me, she jumps off the couch. "Oh my god, Jenny, I was so worried!"

"Why?"

"I didn't know where you were going or anything. I wanted to make sure you were okay! I didn't hear from you! Jon tried to contact you, too."

"Don't worry about it. I had my ringer turned off last night."

"Jenny, I'm so sorry," Kathy says, coming over to me. "I should have been upfront with you right away. I was stupid to hide it from you. I recommended Jon to you purely because he's a great agent. He helped me a lot with building up a solid body of work to go after actual roles, like this soap opera. And when I saw him bringing you flowers and being kind to you… it just brought up all these bad emotions," she goes on, rambling, her skin flushed. "I couldn't stand to think I had chased you off. I had the best intentions. I just messed up. I'm sorry."

I put my hand on her shoulder, trying to give her some comfort. "It's okay. Truly. I slept on it and I understand how… tangled emotions can get. But you helped me move forward when I didn't realize I needed to and would never have thought to. I can't hate you for being mad because you thought your ex was moving on. I shouldn't have thought of Jon as anything but an agent. Especially seeing as he didn't consider me as anything else but a client," I add, somewhat bitterly.

Kathy opened her mouth to say something but then shut it and shakes her head. "You should really speak to Jon. He called me, worried about you, trying to get a hold of you."

"It can wait. I should honestly find another agent."

"Oh, Jenny, please reconsider it."

I wave my hand. "If you know of anyone, let me know, okay? I should probably get ready for this audition. I've been so caught up in this stuff."

Kathy watches as I head to my room and calls out, "Jenny, please call Jon."

I don't call Jon. I do listen to his voicemail though.

"Jenny. Please call me. I want to clear this up with you. What you heard... what happened with Kathy and me. Are you with Rich?"

The other voicemail is from Kathy. She has sent me two texts as well but there is nothing else from Jon. I try to push that from my mind and focus on my audition instead. If I nail this part, I can find another agent. They would want to represent someone on a show, surely? It puts a spark in me to keep trying my hardest.

When I am acting out the scenes in my room, this time not caring if Kathy hears me, I feel my mind wiped clean from worries. It is different than when I was with Rich. My mind is blank but fills with a desire to feel him and be around him. This is a pure focus on the words and the emotion I can put behind them. Even if Rich is in the audition, I won't let someone I know being there throw me off.

<<◇>>

As Kathy and I drive to the audition on Monday, I try not to let my nerves show. I have spent the entire weekend focusing purely on preparing for this audition. I know I am going to see Jon as well as Rich. I can't let that ruin my focus.

"Are you nervous?" I ask Kathy, wondering if someone who's been through this several times already can still be nervous.

"Always, although I have managed to come up with ways to handle my nerves. When I first started out, it used to tear me down completely. The fear was insane."

"What did you do to fix it?"

"I thought of the worst moment in my life and just let it sink in me. Wash over me, really. I sat there in this shitty memory from my past and felt the fear from it. And then I began to grapple with it and fight with it. Instead of running from those emotions, I faced them head on and used them to my advantage . I fought my fear and I won. Now when I think of that memory, I feel in control of it. I take the essence of it and apply it to the auditions."

"Wow," I breathe. "That's impressive."

I wish I could do something like that. But anytime I let myself go back to that moment with my pregnant belly and Robbs looming over me, my entire brain shuts down. I don't think I could live in that moment. Going through it once was enough.

"It is terrible at first. But the power you get from it and the ability to put other aspects in control of your life is awesome."

I study Kathy, feeling curious. I realize that even though we live together, the two of us have been so wrapped up in our own lives that I don't even know a lot of what makes Kathy tick. I make myself a promise to find out more once this audition is over.

We pull into the same building as before. I brace myself and follow Kathy inside the first floor. A couple of other girls I recognize from the first audition head toward the elevator. I wonder how many out of the fifty original girls they have called back.

"Jenny!"

I turn around to see Jon over in a corner by the window, waving me over.

"I'll wait for you upstairs," Kathy replies tactfully. Before I can stop her, she darts off toward the elevator.

Knowing I can't avoid Jon anymore, I walk over to him. He has bags under his eyes and looks as if he has dressed in a hurry.

"I have to hurry. My audition is soon."

"I know. But I need to talk to you about what happened."

"Why? I know everything already. Listen, I'm probably going to try to find another agent."

Jon's eyes widen in surprise. "Jenny, please don't be rash."

"I'm not. I just don't feel like having a person represent me who tried to make their ex-girlfriend jealous."

Surprise flickers over his face and Jon suddenly laughs. "Jenny, you think…? Oh my god, I can't believe you think I was trying to make Kathy jealous."

His laughter pisses me off. I bristle and turn to leave.

"Glad you find it funny. Let me know how the audition goes, okay?"

"No, Jenny, I'm sorry, wait!"

But I ignore him and head toward the elevator. My heart pounds in my chest and it isn't because of the upcoming audition. I am shaken by how strongly I felt when I saw him. Yes, Jon laughing as if I am stupid and naïve has rubbed me the wrong way. But just seeing him again has dragged up my feelings for him. I hate myself for it. He doesn't feel the same. I have Rich. What is wrong with me? Why do I always get hung up on bad men?

The elevator doors open, and I decide I need to try to calm myself and focus. Not because I am going to have a panic attack, like that time at the grocery store that feels like centuries ago, but just because I want to make sure I'm not going to take this bad energy into the audition with me. I turn down a small hallway and head toward the ladies' restroom. At the same time, someone comes out of the men's room. I realize it is Rich.

"Jenny. Hey, the auditions start soon."

"Yeah, just have to use the restroom," I reply, pointing to the door.

"Well, it's great seeing you again. I had a great time last night."

I try not to blush and look over my shoulder. I don't want a bunch of people hearing that I slept with Rich last night and knowing he's partially involved with casting. Rich notices and he laughs.

"Jenny, I wouldn't worry about that. Everyone on the casting team knows they're doing me a solid."

I blink. "What?"

Rich shifts and lowers his voice. "You know, getting you a callback because of our status."

"What?" I repeat, feeling like an idiot.

"You know." He motions between the two of us. "Anyway, I'm sure you'll be great."

"Wait," I say slowly. "Are you saying they didn't want to call me back originally?"

"I just suggested they give you a callback. They were worried about your inexperience, but you take direction great. They could mold you. Anyway, I gotta go. Talk to you later."

Rich moves past me and heads down the hall. I watch him go, all my confidence drained. I *did* only get the callback because I'm seeing Rich. Another thought strikes me. Would I have even had a chance at all if I didn't get involved with him?

Eyes filling with tears, I slam my way into the restroom.

Chapter Thirteen

For the first time since I moved to Hollywood, I want to go back home. I don't want to stay here anymore. Despair clings to me as I sit in the stall, staring at the door. Confusion reigns inside of me. Part of me wants to blow off the audition completely. Another part of me wants to go in there and nail it. Show them that even if Rich did have hand in getting me a second audition, I deserve that spot.

I can't shake the thought that Rich has gotten me the callback because I slept with him. Kathy has told me multiple times that Hollywood is all about who you know and your connections. But I don't want to be known as the girl who has slept around for a spot on a fucking soap opera.

I close my eyes, feeling the familiar surge of anxiety rise in me. The whole thing with Jon still has me rattled. Seeing him today has made me so upset. And then after running into Rich and seeing how casually he tells me that the callback is due to him makes my heart ache.

My phone vibrates in my purse and I slip it out. There is a text from Kathy asking where I am. I bite my bottom lip. *I should just do the audition.* I put my phone away. Get it over with. I have practiced all weekend. It seems a shame to waste it because of what Rich has said. Then I'll decide if I am moving away afterward.

Taking a shuddering breath and trying to keep my emotions in check, I stand up. I am still going to try my best in this audition. I head out into the hallway and to the waiting room. There are about fifteen other hopefuls waiting, including the woman who looked on the verge of tears the first audition.

Kathy waves me over and I sit down. "Hey, you okay? They already called the first woman in."

"I'm fine," I lie and force a smile. "Just had to calm my nerves."

Kathy relaxes, obviously believing my story, which makes me feel a little better. If I can act well enough to fool Kathy, maybe I'm not as raw and terrible as I think I am. She doesn't ask about Jon, luckily, and instead goes back to reviewing her lines.

This time I am called before her. I give her hand a squeeze and head into the audition room. The same people are there from last time. Amanda gives me a small smile. Rich looks at me as though he doesn't know who I am. *What a professional.* I try to control my irritation. I am not sure yet if I even have a right to be mad at Rich, who probably just thinks he is helping me out. *Think about it after the audition.*

I try to block everyone else out. I throw myself into the first scene. The rest of the audition is a blur. I focus only on myself and what emotions I can put into the scene.

When I finish, Mr. Grant scribbles something down on a piece of paper and then looks up at me. "Thank you. That will be all for now."

Everyone has blank faces, including Rich. I leave the room, heading back toward the elevator. My heart is pounding. I have no idea how I did on the audition but I know that I have tried my very best. I have taken my swirling emotions and focused them. *I did all I could do, especially given the circumstances.* I step into the lobby to wait for Kathy.

Finally getting back into the apartment, I let out a sigh. I suddenly feel exhausted. Waiting for Kathy took another hour. I am running on high emotions and want to nap. She looks tired, too.

"How long does it usually take to find out?" I ask her.

"Anywhere from three days to weeks. Not sure. All we can do is wait. I'm sure you did great though."

I fiddle with the skirt I am wearing as I sit down on the couch. "Kathy, can I ask you a question? It isn't about Jon and you," I add quickly when I see her face.

She relaxes a little and sits down. "Sure."

"It's about Rich. I know Jon and Rich had a falling out. But depending on who you ask, you hear different things. I wasn't sure who to listen to."

"I have to admit I didn't interact with Rich a lot. Jon was representing me right around the time Rich was leaving. So I can't really offer much of an unbiased opinion. Just what Jon told me about how he thought Rich took advantage of some of the clients or would have sex with them in exchange for parts."

"Do people really… I mean, do they do that on purpose? Have sex with someone for a part?"

Kathy leans back on the couch. "Oh, yeah. Anything to get ahead in this city," She looks at me. "Why, did Rich tell you he'd get you the soap opera part if you slept with him?"

I shake my head. "No. I guess I'm just a little wary about everything in this town. I'm thinking about maybe moving back home."

Her eyes widen in surprise. "What? Jenny, you can't! You're already doing so well!"

"Things just feel messy. I don't know if this life is for me after all."

Kathy reaches for my hand. "Jenny, I know you went through a lot of pain and torment before you moved out here. You've been doing so well since you got here, truly. If you're upset about Jon, then switch agents. I'll help. But you have talent. It seems like such a shame to leave right now when you seem so focused on things."

She has a point as much as I don't want to admit it. Ever since moving to Hollywood, I haven't been able to think about my previous pain. Seeing a child doesn't bring a panic attack like it did before. Besides some nightmares about Robbs, I have been completely focused on what life is handing out to me.

Kathy goes on, "If you don't want to keep going after acting, then don't. We'll find another job for you. At least think about it."

"I'll think about it," I concede.

Kathy smiles. "Great. I'm so glad. Maybe we'll go do something soon, just the two of us, to relax, okay? We deserve it."

"That sounds nice," I say and I mean it.

After we finish talking, I find myself curling up in bed. My head is ready to burst with so many thoughts. All I want is to sleep for a while.

After my nap, I find myself going over my bank account. If I keep slumming it like I am doing and focus on paying the basics, such as rent, I still can only go one more month without any sort of income. *If I don't get this role, I will definitely need to get a job on the side.*

My phone suddenly goes off. It's Rich. I bite my bottom lip, debate answering it or ignoring it. Finally, I decide to answer. I can't see Rich anymore. I am getting involved with him way too quickly. I don't want to be part of his "girls", getting auditions because of what I do with him.

Rich wants to see me, so I agree to meet him at a coffee shop close by. Kathy is curled up in bed, sleeping off what she calls her "audition hangover". I dress quickly and pull my hair up in a loose ponytail, throwing only a little makeup on. Is this a break-up? I am not sure what to think of it as. I just know I need to get everything back in control.

<<◇>>

Rich is looking around the coffee shop distastefully when I step inside. It is very small and rundown. Probably not what he is used to in Beverly Hills. As I watch him look at the menu with a frown, I try to think of what I like so much about him. Everything I come up with seems to be linked to superficial things – his looks, his house, his air success. I shake my head to clear my thoughts and go over to him.

"There you are. Have you been here before? They don't even have soy milk," Rich says in a put-off tone, looking back at the menu.

"Yeah, they just sell regular coffee," I reply dryly.

We each order a coffee and sit down at one of the small tables in the back. The place is decorated with things that look like they came from a storage unit. Trip-hop plays over the speakers, giving the entire café a sort of dream vibe to it. I find myself enjoying it, even though Rich is hating every second.

"I'm glad you answered my call. I wanted to talk to you about the audition," Rich says as he dumps a sugar packet into his coffee.

"Me, too, actually."

Rich leans forward as if he is going to tell me a secret. "It's between you and Kathy."

I freeze. "What?"

"Yeah, they really loved the passion you brought to the audition. But your friend is polished and really on top of things. They liked that she had experience as well." He shrugs.

"Kathy deserves it," I say automatically.

"Do you really believe that? Listen, they are leaning toward Kathy. But I'd be more prone to helping you out if you, you know…"

I stare at him. "What?"

"If you'd like to come over and spend the night." He raises his eyebrows.

"Are you asking me to sleep with you for the part?" I reply, barely able to keep my voice to a whisper.

"What? Don't tell me you thought the other times were because we had slept together." He waves his hand. "No, I merely helped you out with getting a callback because we were hanging out."

"And what, this is a formal notice?" I reply icily.

"What's the big deal? I thought we had an understanding."

"How the hell did we have an understanding?"

Rich looks surprised. "I showed you around the city. I could tell you wanted to fuck. That's fine, I like throwing girls a bone every now and then." He grins. "But I mean… I just wanted to show you that we were friends with the callback. That wasn't because we slept together."

"But to get the part I have to sleep with you? That's what you're telling me?"

"I just mean I can scratch your back if you scratch mine."

The ice melts and rage overcomes me. *Stupid! So stupid to fall for this guy!* I stand up, wanting to throw my coffee at him, but he's not worth the effort. I am seeing red. He *threw me a bone* by fucking me the first time. Gave me the callback because we are "friends". But now if I want the part, I am supposed to sleep with him again?

"And what about the night at your home?" I ask him through clenched teeth.

"Fun between friends. I thought you knew we weren't exclusive."

"I know I was just one of your 'girls'. But I'm not sleeping with you to get a part. You misread everything that happened between us. I slept with you because I liked you. I wasn't expecting you to get a callback for me or do me any favors. And I am not sleeping with you for a role. Go fuck yourself."

I turn sharply on my heel and storm out of the coffee shop. Rich doesn't come after me. I am fuming! I agreed to see Rich to tell him I can't see him anymore. Instead, he tries to get me to fuck him for a soap opera role. My knuckles are turning white from my angry fists. Kathy deserves that role. If it comes down between sleeping with Rich to get it and Kathy getting it, then she needs to get that role.

I have taken care of Rich, even if it was in a way I hated. I am going to lose the soap opera role, which means I am going to need find a job soon and fast. Next, I have to figure out how to handle seeing Jon. He is still my agent. Do I want to keep him as an agent? Will I be able to move on from my feelings with him?

I decide I will give him a call.

Jon agrees to meet me at the cheap taco shop across the street from the apartment.

"Traffic is brutal today so I'll come to you to make things easier. I'm about to leave the office anyway," he says on the phone.

I have agreed because I feel that I may have been too rash with him the last time we had spoken. And with Rich being an absolute asshole, how can things get worse today? No, better to clear the air with Jon and see if I need a new agent.

I head over to the small taco shop. I can see Jon already inside, drinking a soda. He looks out the window and waves when he sees me. I step inside.

"Hey. I was waiting for you before I ordered anything," Jon says as he stands up, making his way to the counter.

As we order our food, I look at him out of the corner of my eye. Jon is wearing his glasses and just a T-shirt and jeans. I have never seen him look so casual before. He looks incredibly handsome. My chest tightens when I think about how I had been falling for him before everything had gotten so messy.

Once we get our food and sit down in the booth, Jon speaks first.

"I'm glad you called me. I feel like our wires have been crossed since the night we went to the restaurant down the street. I hadn't meant for things to happen like that."

"I could have handled it better myself," I admit. "Not been so hard on you and listened to you. I cut you off in the lobby, too. I shouldn't have."

"I understand why you did though. I know you overheard… Kathy and me talking about our past."

"I lost my cool. Completely. It was lame of me. What you went through with Kathy is your own past. Not mine."

"Right." Jon shifts in his seat. "But the other thing I said… about how I have no feelings for you…," Jon's voice almost trails off as he's gathering his thoughts.

Did I read everything wrong? I think to myself. I mean, I used to think that I could read guys pretty well. But I could have just fucked it all up.

"I just said that because Kathy had been so upset about me moving on from her. I just tried to diffuse the situation, and I handled it terribly. I'm sorry."

I peer up at him, my heart starting to beat quickly. "Does this mean that you're… you're saying you were lying?"

For the first time ever, I see Jon blush. "I was lying. I am interested in you. I have a great time with you. I want to see this how far it goes."

Relief sweeps through me. Jon *is* interested in me. I haven't misread the signs. I smile at him.

"That's great," I breathe. "I'm happy to hear that."

"You're…?"

"Interested… Yes. I still am interested."

Jon smiles and crams his mouth full of a bite from his burrito to try to hide it. When he swallows, he looks thoughtful.

"I probably shouldn't be your agent anymore. Conflict of interest."

"Yeah, I was thinking the same thing."

"We'll see what happens with this soap opera audition and then go from there."

Part of me wants to tell Jon what has happened with Rich. But at the last second, I change my mind. I feel stupid to tell him that I haven't listened to his warnings about Rich and had fallen into his arms not once, but twice. How could I have been blinded by someone like Rich? After what I have gone through with Paul and Robbs, I hoped I would avoid this sort of shit forever.

Telling Jon how badly I had fucked up makes me embarrassed. I can't bear to see the look on his face when I tell him I had been used by Rich. No, better just to let it fade away. When I don't get the audition, we can move on from the entire mess.

"Sounds good," I say, and I smile.

Chapter Fourteen

When my phone goes off early Monday morning, I jolt awake. I was having another nightmare. The same one as always. Robbs' hands on me and the stairs raising up to meet my face. The pain in my stomach. Then the dream melts into something else. Maggie is crying somewhere. I am running through a house that just seems to grow larger and larger. Every room I check is empty. All I can hear is her crying. Her cries grow louder and louder by the time I finally find a room that has a crib in it. As I run over to check the crib, I suddenly wake up.

My phone keeps ringing. My heart is pounding as I look around my tiny bedroom, trying to catch my breath. I am dripping with sweat, as if I have actually been running. I see it is Jon. I pick it up.

"Hello?" I try to calm myself down.

"Hey, did I wake you?"

"No," I lie. "What's up?" Breathing normally now.

"I heard from the soap opera today. They decided to go with someone else for the role. I'm sorry, Jenny. I know you tried your best. But they just wanted someone with more experience."

I already knew I wasn't going to get the role but tried to sound upset. "Well, I tried my hardest. Can't win them all. I'll call you later, okay?"

I hang up, trying to still my racing heart. The nightmare was so vivid. It feels as if I was actually running around trying to find out where my daughter is. I wish Jon had waited a few extra seconds before he ended up calling me. I want to know if Maggie was in the crib.

It doesn't matter, even if she was. She isn't here anymore, Jenny. I know that. I know I'll never see or hold my daughter. She is gone from this world. The closest I can get to her will be in dreams. I will fight to see her in dreams.

I think back to what Kathy has said about living in her fear and using it to get herself through the auditions. The thought of sinking into the bad memories of my past and going through them terrify me. It is easier to run from them and pretend that they never happened. The thought of facing them head on and living through them again is too much to bear.

I slink out of bed and into the shower, scrubbing myself so raw that my skin is bright red. I allow the hot water to roll over me. I imagine the dream is rolling off of me and going down the drain where I don't have to think about it anymore.

Once I feel okay, I finish the shower and step out, thinking about the audition. I knew I wasn't going to get it after I refused to sleep with Rich for the part. But I have to stop beating myself up over it as well. I fell into Rich's trap. I got lured in by his good looks and his charm. I ended things with him because I wanted to but I am refusing to let him suck me back in again. I haven't heard from him since I told him to fuck off anyway.

"Jenny? Jenny?" Kathy calls.

I quickly wrap a towel around me and poke my head out. Kathy is standing in the kitchen, positively glowing. I know the news before she says it.

"I got the part!" she squeals.

"You did? That's amazing!" I cry. "I would hug you but…," Kathy can see I got out of the shower, my wet hair dripping water all over the floor.

Kathy laughs. "It's okay. Finish getting ready."

I duck back into the bathroom. Kathy stands outside the door and tells me about how she has just gotten the call.

"Apparently it came down to me and one other girl. But one of the casting directors didn't think she would work well with the cast, so they picked me!"

I bite my tongue as I comb out my hair. Is that the bullshit Rich has told them? I feel unnerved by the entire experience. I know Mr. Grant and the others liked how well I took direction. But the entire audition and callback was only due to Rich. Am I really talented or just a complete flop? I feel insecure. But I refuse to let any of this ruin Kathy's moment.

"That's amazing!" I cry through the door. "You must be so thrilled!"

"This steady gig means I can take a break from the infomercials I kept getting cast in not to mention those terrible B-movies. My last one was about aliens who took over beavers' bodies. I mean, really?"

"Wow that does sound terrible," I reply, finally dressed and opening the door.

Kathy laughs. "I know!" Then her face falls. "Oh, honey, I'm sorry. Here I am blabbing away when that means you didn't get the part."

"I'm sure Jon will call me any minute to tell me. It's fine, honestly. You deserved it more than me."

"You have talent. I feel confident that you can do it."

"Well, they will probably make a sequel to your alien beaver movie, right? I can play your sister or something," I joke.

Upon seeing I wasn't angry, Kathy relaxes and pulls me in for a hug. I am truly happy for her. She deserves the part. My phone goes off again in my bedroom.

"It's probably Jon," I say.

Kathy nods, darting off, holding her phone and getting ready to call her family about the news.

It is Jon calling. I answer.

"Jenny," His tone is odd and my grasp on the phone tightens. "Can you come down here? Right away?"

"Right now? I can see —"

"Please hurry. At my office."

He hangs up. I find myself staring at the phone in confusion. I grab my purse and tell Kathy what is going on. She insists I use her car.

"I don't need it until two this afternoon," she says to me, covering her phone as she speaks to her parents. "So just have it back by then."

I say thanks and dart out toward her car. A sick feeling has formed in my stomach. Something about Jon's tone had seemed so different than usual. What could he possibly need to see me right away for? I try to think if there is something I am missing, something in the big picture that I should make sure to discuss with him but nothing comes to mind.

Naturally I hit traffic. Any Zen I have been feeling is quickly wiped away by rage as I wish people learned how to drive. It takes what feels like ages to get to his office. I try to imagine what would make Jon sound so stressed out but I am not sure what it can be. Maybe I am reading too much into his tone. It could be that he just wants to see me about the audition. I did sound strange on the phone when he called me the first time. My mind had still been in the nightmare. Someone could take that as me freaking out and wanting to be alone.

I finally get to his office building and park the car. I try to control my breathing but I can't shake the feeling that I am going to get bad news. *What else could get out of control?* With a racing heart, I make my way inside of the lobby. It is almost empty. There are a few other agents housed in the same building, and I see one girl in a corner, fighting with someone on her phone.

I get into the elevator and anxiously wait till the doors open for me to step out into the waiting room of his office.

His assistant is there, pink neon nails and big hair. She smiles at me. "Oh, I'll let him know you're here."

She buzzes in the back and nods a couple of times before lowering the phone. "He'll see you now."

I nod and follow her down the hallway. She doesn't seem stressed out. Maybe this isn't a big deal at all. Wouldn't she know if it is something truly bad? I know I am grasping at straws at this point.

I can't really think of anything else as I step inside his office. Jon is at the computer, a frown on his face. My heart is racing. I want to shake whatever he has to tell me out of him.

"Jenny," he says as his assistant leaves, shutting the door behind us.

"Hey. I came as quickly as I could. What's going on? Is this about the soap opera? Because I'm fine. I'm glad that Kathy got it." I barely finish what I'm saying when Jon cuts me off.

"It isn't about the soap opera. Sit down."

"Oh. Okay." I sit down, suddenly feeling like a school kid about to get in trouble from the principal.

"I got something in the mail today."

I nod, not following what in the world Jon is talking about.

"I wish you would have told me about this."

"Told you about what?" I ask, starting to feel incredibly stupid and slightly annoyed.

Jon sighs. "Jenny, please. Don't make me say it out loud."

"I honestly don't know what the hell you are talking about." I am starting to lose my temper now.

Jon rubs his eyes and suddenly I am terrified about what he is going to tell me.

"The sex tape, Jenny. I wish you would you have told me about the sex tape."

-To be continued in Book 2-

If you enjoyed this title, I would appreciate your leaving a review of the book. Good reviews encourage an author to write as well as help books to sell. Good reviews can be just a few short sentences describing what you liked about the book without having a spoiler. If you could spend 30 seconds writing a review, I would appreciate it: you can review this title right now at your favorite retailer.

133

Here is a preview of the **next story** you may also enjoy:

THE FEAR crushes me. I feel it on my chest, alive and burrowing its way inside of me. I gasp for air and spin around. Robbs lurks behind me, somewhere in the shadows. He calls my name. His throat is raw and hoarse. He calls my name again, and I scream, kicking off the ground with my heels. The world spins around me, and all I can think about is my child. I have to protect Maggie.

But Robbs comes out of the darkness. His hands are outstretched. I scream again, wildly, hoping someone will come for me. But his hands press against my back, and the world swirls in different shades of red as I connect with the stairs. I fall down them, and pain lances through me like a sharp blade.

Suddenly I stop falling. My vision goes in and out. Someone cackles over me – a sick grin twisting their face. More faces appear, laughing at me. They are clowns, I realize, as the pain makes my stomach ache brutally.

One more face appears. Robbs looms over me with a sick grin. He lets out another loud laugh and suddenly everything fades to black.

I awaken with a start, jolting upright in my bed. My fingers are wrapped up in my T-shirt, and I am panting. My entire body is covered in a cold sweat, my hair is stuck to my face. I let out a trembling breath, looking around the room in a panic, trying to remember where I am. A wild glance over at the night table shows me it is a little past three in the morning. I feel groggy and sick, as if I am going to vomit. My eyes land on chocolates on my dresser, and I remember Kathy gave them to me in an attempt to cheer me up.

Kathy. I am in Hollywood. I remember everything in quick flashing images. Moving to Hollywood to try my luck at acting. Meeting Jon and Rich and quickly becoming torn between the two of them. Jon and Kathy dating. Rich and I sleeping together. Losing out on a part in a soap opera only to find out that Kathy landed one. Jon calling me in to tell me he had received a sex tape from Robbs.

I shut my eyes tightly. I have been trying so hard to move on from my past. The terrible things that I have done to people, like Kiara and Paul. I remember how I used my pregnancy to get what I wanted out of them. I was a terrible person. Since Robbs pushed me down the stairs, I have been trying to be on the straight and narrow. Coming to terms with the fact I had suffered at the hands of an emotional and physical relationship is not easy. Yet it is even harder when that person returns to torment you.

I get out of bed, padding my way toward the bathroom. Kathy is fast asleep on the other side of our small apartment, which we've nicknamed "The Dollhouse". Her first day of shooting on the soap set is in the morning. A part of me wishes it was me who was heading to the studio, but it would have meant having to sleep with Rich for the part.

I step inside the bathroom and splash cold water on my face, trying to forget the nightmare. It is the same thing every night – the same terrible dream, a strange mix of memory and twisted horror movie imagery – that has kept me exhausted and out of sorts the past week. I look at myself in the mirror. The moon casts a shadow along the bathroom, making my features look haggard.

A week ago, Robbs returned to my life. The asshole had sent Jon a sex tape. He hadn't said anything to Jon, just sent the tape. But as soon as I looked over and saw a scene from it, briefly, in the privacy of my bedroom after Jon sent me the email, I threw up. The sight of Paul and I entangled together was too much to bear. The threat is clear – *I have this tape. I can ruin you at any moment. You thought you escaped but you will always be under my thumb.*

Robbs and I had been so pleased with the plan originally. It was the perfect way to set-up Paul and put Kiara in her place. I had detested her for so long. It clouded my judgement. But now that lapse in judgement was coming back to bite me in the ass, big time.

I splash more water on my face to keep a panic attack from blooming. I have been locked up in my room the past week. Finally, Kathy asked what was going on and I told her. She knows about Robbs and filling in the blanks is easier than telling Jon the entire story. How do I tell him that I slept with Paul in a scheme to get back at Kiara? Why don't you just paint *Terrible Person* on my head and be done with it? My feelings for Jon are so strong that if he decides not to speak to me anymore or drop me as a client, I would be heartbroken.

I turn off the faucet and sit down on the bathroom floor. The tiles are icy cold, and I draw my knees to my chest, closing my eyes. My past will forever haunt me. I could move anywhere in the world, and Robbs would be there, looming over me, a horrifying specter of my past.

I feel frozen, unsure how to plan out my next move. Rich had even called me yesterday although I can't fathom why. Last time we hung out, he told me I had to sleep with him again for a soap opera part, and I told him to fuck off. Part of me couldn't face Jon. I was unsure what to say to him or how to act around him. As my agent, he would want to discuss the tape. As a possible love interest, he would want to know more about the tape. It was a lose-lose situation.

I make my way back to bed. I tell myself I will call Rich in the morning. At least I won't have to explain anything to him. And if he is an asshole, then perhaps letting out my pent-up aggression on him might serve me well.

If you enjoyed this sample then look for **Star Bright, Book 2**.

Here is a preview of the **first book of the series** that started it all:

**Fifty Recipes For Disaster: A New Adult Romance
Series - Book 1**

"**ALL RIGHT**, chefs, you have ninety seconds to get
your food plated and presented. If your dish isn't ready,
you will automatically be eliminated."

My cooking instructor, Chef Michelle Lee, walks
through the room, examining our stations. My fellow
cooking students and I are competing for the chance to
enter another competition. The winner of today's
cooking challenge will get the chance to compete for a
full-time apprenticeship at Fission, one of Austin's
hottest restaurants.

I'm not confident in many aspects of my life, but I
know I dominate in the kitchen. I begin plating my dish
just as Chef Lee approaches my station.

"Your food presents beautifully as usual, Kiara,"
she tells me with a smile. "If it tastes as good as it
looks, you've got this in the bag," she adds with a soft
whisper.

The instructors at *Le Cordon Bleu College of
Culinary Arts* aren't supposed to show favoritism to
their students, but Chef Lee keeps a soft spot for me.
Along with being one of my teachers, she's also my
faculty adviser, and she knows the unusual
circumstances that brought me to the school.

"Time's up," she calls out to the class. "Place your
finished plates on the head table."

I walk my plate to the front of the room and place it on top of the placard that holds my student ID number. My classmates follow suit… several of them glare at me after looking at my dish. I am delighted, knowing they're all both jealous and impressed I was able to execute a well-developed *Cioppino* within the given time frame. My rich seafood stew is accompanied by fresh sourdough loaves. I examine my classmates' dishes and feel my chances of winning are good.

"Clear away your stations," Chef Lee directs. "Chef Lawton will be here shortly to judge your plates, and I don't want any evidence of who made what on display when he arrives."

Chef Lawton is the *sous* chef at Fission and the judge of this stage of the apprenticeship competition. I clear my station quickly and then I take a seat at the front of the room. I want to be able to see Chef Lawton's expressions as he tastes each dish.

As I sit nervously in my chair, my classmates finish clearing their stations. I can tell everyone else is just as anxious as I am… we've received plenty of critiques from our instructors but this will be the first time a professional chef from a restaurant will be tasting our food. The door of the classroom opens and a tall man wearing a black chef's jacket enters the room.

"Chef Lawton, it's so lovely to see you," Chef Lee welcomes him. "I can't tell you how excited we are to participate in this competition."

"We're excited as well," Chef Lawton replies. "We're always looking for new, innovative chefs at

Fission. I'm looking forward to tasting the dishes and welcoming one of your students into the final leg of the competition. I see that all of the plates are ready. If it's all right with you, I'll get started."

"Of course," Chef Lee agrees.

I try not to hold my breath as I watch Chef Lawton sample each of the plates. I feel encouraged when he reaches mine. Instead of sampling one bite and moving on, he holds the broth in his mouth for a moment, and then tastes each type of seafood in turn. The expression on his face tells me that my stew is perfect, and I say a silent prayer I haven't been out-cooked by any of my classmates.

"First off, I'd like to say this is an impressive display," the seasoned chef begins. "Everything on this table is up to par with the level of skill and talent I expect to see from second-year students. That being said, there is a clear winner. One chef not only executed a delicious dish, but also added a few subtle, original touches that showed innovation and creativity."

Adrenaline rushes through me as he moves to stand behind my dish. "Who created this *Cioppino*?" he asks.

I blush involuntarily as I raise my hand.

"And what is your name, Chef?"

"Kiara Sands," I reply, trying to mask the excitement in my voice.

"Well, Chef Sands, it's an honor to welcome you to the next stage of the competition. I look forward to tasting more of your food as the weeks progress. I am needed back at Fission, but Chef Lee will provide you with the details of your new position." He turns to the rest of the class. "To the rest of you, don't be discouraged. You all provided me with excellent dishes, and you have bright futures ahead of you."

"Thank you, Chef," the class responds in unison.

Chef Lawton makes a quick exit, and Chef Lee takes his place behind the head table. "Excellent work today, class. You're dismissed until tomorrow," she announces. My classmates gather their things and leave the room… I stay behind to talk to Chef Lee.

"Kiara, I'm so proud of you." She beams once we are alone. "As you know, there will be two other chefs competing with you at Fission. You're the only one who's been selected from *Le Cordon Bleu*, and I know you'll represent us well." She moves to her desk and pulls a large package from her bottom drawer. "Here is your apprenticeship packet. You'll receive your Fission jacket when you report for work tomorrow morning. If you have any questions, or just need someone to talk to, you know where to reach me."

"This seems like a wonderful dream, and part of me is afraid that I'll wake up any minute now," I confess.

Chef Lee gives me a maternal smile. "This is a dream, Kiara. It's your dream. And you're well on *your* way to achieving it."

The information packet Chef Lee presented me with instructs me to be at Fission at 10:00 am. I check my dashboard clock as I pull into the parking lot… 9:40 am. I feel smug, knowing I'm probably the first of the three competitors to arrive. I check my makeup in the rear-view mirror before exiting my car.

Fission is housed in a modern brick building in East Austin, one of the city's burgeoning hipster areas. The area gives off a relaxed, laid-back vibe, but I know the kitchen of Fission will be anything but.

I push open the heavy, solid oak door and am greeted by a pixy-sized hostess with spiked, lavender hair.

"Table for one?" she asks me brightly.

"No," I reply nervously. "My name is Kiara Sands. I'm supposed to start work today."

"Oh! You're one of the newbies!" She says warmly. "I'm Megan. It's a pleasure to meet you. The other two are already here. I'll show you to their table."

Damn it! I'd been so sure I'd make the best impression by arriving first, and here I am, the last of the apprentices to report for our first day.

Megan seems to sense my disappointment. "Don't worry. Paul doesn't give a shit how early people show up. As long as you're here when you're scheduled, you'll be fine. And you haven't missed anything. The other two have just been sitting alone since they got here," she offers reassuringly.

"Thank you for that," I say half-heartedly. As I follow Megan through the restaurant, I'm struck by the eclectic, well-placed décor. All of the tables are made of the same polished oak as the front door. The water goblets on the tabletops are tinted in hues of blue, green, and rose… a selection of art from all around the world adorns the walls. The ambiance is on the right side of the fine line between cozy and overwhelming. The restaurant offers a large main dining room, with smaller, more private rooms on each side.

"This is a beautiful place," I say as Megan leads me toward the back of the main room.

"It is," she agrees. "Paul handled all of the decorating himself. He says that Austin is a melting pot, and he wants all of our customers to feel at home when they dine here."

I'm about to comment on how successfully that goal had been achieved when we arrive at a table occupied by a beautiful blonde woman and a swarthy man with sandy blond hair. A pot of coffee and three cups sit on the table.

"Kiara Sands, this is Jenny Foster and Robbs Martin," Megan introduces us. She checks her watch before speaking again. "It's a quarter to ten, so I imagine that Paul will be out shortly. I suggest you get fully caffeinated and enjoy this time off your feet. It will be the last one for today," she warns with a friendly, knowing tone.

I take a seat in the chair next to Jenny as Megan moves back to the hostess station. "It's a pleasure to meet you both," I offer.

"It's a pleasure to meet you too," Robbs replies. "Congratulations on making it this far in the competition. And I'd like to apologize right now for how thoroughly I'm going to kick both of your asses. This job is mine." He speaks with a blend of arrogance and sarcasm, and I can tell immediately that Robbs and I are not going to get along.

Personal relationships are something I struggle with. In my experience, there's no point in getting close to someone who will inevitably let you down. I prefer to keep my head down and focus on getting my job done. As Chef Lee said yesterday, I have a dream and I'm well on my way to achieving it. I'll be damned if I let Robbs or anyone else get in my way.

"Just ignore Robbs," Jenny advises me. "He thinks that he's God's gift to food... women too, probably." She giggles. "So Kiara, what's your story? Which campus were you plucked from?"

"I'm in my second year at *Le Cordon Bleu*," I answer with pride. In my opinion, *Le Cordon Bleu* is the best culinary school in the area—it's also the hardest to get in to. Jenny seems impressed by my background, but Robbs laughs and dismisses it immediately.

"The *Bleu* is all right, I guess," he snorts, "if you're happy being complacent and doing everything old-school."

"I wasn't aware that being classically trained is a bad thing," I reply shortly. "Tell me, what culinary Mecca do you hail from?"

"*Escoffier*," he answers with a cocky smile. "You know, where all of the innovative, cutting-edge people attend. Three of my instructors were nominated for the James Beard award. So like I said, no hard feelings, but I'm going to kick both of your asses. *Escoffier* specializes in farm-to-table cuisine, so I'm exactly the kind of chef Fission is looking for."

I dismiss his statement with a glare. While the *Auguste Escoffier School of Culinary Arts* is reputed for turning out fantastic chefs, in some culinary circles it's dismissed as a hipster college that prioritizes food trends over basic technique and skill.

I don't feel like debating the merits of my education with Robbs, so I turn to Jenny. "And where do you go?" I ask pleasantly.

"The Art Institute," she replies. "I'm still not positive that cooking is my life's passion. I wanted to go to a college that offers other programs, in case I decided to change my major."

"If you're not sure that you want to be a chef, then what the fuck are you doing here?" Robbs asks hotly. "You should give your spot to someone who knows that this is what they want."

Jenny's green eyes fill with both anger and embarrassment, and I can tell she's fumbling for a response.

"I don't agree with that at all," I say warmly. "What better way to find out if you enjoy working in a real kitchen, than by actually doing it?"

"That's exactly what my instructor said when I won this spot," Jenny says with a nod.

"I see how it's going to be," Robbs interjects with more sarcasm. "The two of you are going to band together in 'sisterhood' and gang up on me."

"That's not how it's going to be at all," a firm voice says from behind me. I turn to see one of the most attractive men I've ever laid my eyes on. He's tall, with broad shoulders, blue eyes, and sandy blond hair. He's also wearing a black chef's jacket, identical to the one Chef Lawton wore when he judged my dish. He holds eye contact with me for several moments before he speaks again.

"This competition will come down to one thing and one thing only... the quality of your food. Only one of you will be named my new apprentice, so ganging up on each other won't serve any purpose. I'm Paul Weston, and I'd like to welcome you to my restaurant." He extends his hand to me.

I respond with a firm handshake and a smile. "I'm Kiara Sands. Thank you for this opportunity."

"You're here because you deserve to be. No thanks are necessary," he assures me.

If you enjoyed this sample then look for **Fifty Recipes For Disaster: A New Adult Romance Series - Book 1**.

Here is a preview of **another story** you may enjoy:

Romeo Alpha: A BBW Paranormal Shifter Romance - Book 1 by Darla Dunbar

AMANDA WONDERED how the hell she had gotten so far away from home. When she walked, she usually didn't go past a couple of blocks, but she felt so different today. Something was pushing her further and in a different direction, and she wasn't sure what it was. But she didn't care at the moment, because she just wanted to walk.

Not thinking twice about where she was going, she let her gut instinct give her the direction she needed.

Her grandmother had always told her to go with her gut. She'd said human instinct was better than anything. "Intuition is a girl's best friend," she would say, and then they would both laugh. Talks she and her grandmother had always seemed to pop into her head at the strangest of times, like now.

Here she was, going for a walk, and wondering why she wanted to go in a different direction, and there was her grandmother's voice in her head, propelling her along. Amanda missed her grandmother more with every passing year.

Amanda paused and thought about her life thus far. She had just graduated from college and started working in the local animal hospital, but it wasn't quite like she had thought. She didn't see the care and passion she'd hoped to find in the industry. In the city, being a vet was all about how much money you could make, how many pets you could treat. And, at twenty-four, it was hard to be taken seriously.

Her two female roommates were nice, but they all just went their separate ways. They didn't eat ice cream and watch movies like on *Friends*. They didn't share secrets or even laugh or hang out. They really just slept in the same apartment, and they usually weren't even home at the same time. Except Amanda, that is.

Amanda was always at home, it seemed. She had nowhere else to go, really. The other two girls spent most nights out with their real friends or their boyfriends. Amanda lived a lonely life, but she was happy. At least, she was pretty sure she was happy. After all, she had an upstanding career, and she still had money left over from her savings.

Both her parents had been killed in a car accident years ago. Amanda had graduated from high school with no family there that day or on the day she graduated from college. It was what it was, though, and she knew that her parents watched her from Heaven.

The only positive thing was that her parents had been prepared and had made sure they left enough money and a big enough life insurance policy to help her out. They would be surprised but happy knowing how much that money had helped her in the years after their death. She was proud to say that she was able to live off of it through her college years. She'd never even had to get a job like most kids did. Amanda had been able to focus on her classes.

That freedom wasn't worth it, though. She would have worked three jobs at a time while going to school for one more day with her parents.

However, the account was finally starting to dry up, and she needed to think about what she would do. Sure, she had a new job that could pay her bills, but those loans were piling up with interest. Even a vet job only went so far.

Amanda sighed as she began the trek back toward the house.

Amanda liked her walks in the evening. It helped her to relax, enjoying the quiet time alone. And while Amanda wasn't overweight by any means, it helped slim her waistline, which showed those extra biscuits she liked every now and again.

She turned and began to make her way back to the townhouse she shared with her roommates, but stopped as she heard a noise

A rustling came from behind her, and she turned to see the bushes shaking. Looking over to the other side of the sidewalk, she saw those bushes shake as well. Not wanting to wait around to find out what was behind the leaves, she took off at a run. She swore she heard a growl come from behind her, but she didn't turn to see what was chasing her. That would only slow her down. As she reached the door to her home, she quickly turned the knob and went through headfirst. Shutting the door quickly, she looked out the window. She got a glimpse of a long black furry tail as something ran around to the side of her building.

"What in the world are you doing, Amanda?" Betsy stood there looking at her inquisitively.

"Something was chasing me."

"What?"

"I don't know what it was, but something big and furry was chasing me. I saw a long black tail just now when I walked into the house."

"You mean when you dove into the house?" Betsy's grin faded. "I'll call the game warden. If there is a big animal outside, then none of us need to go out there until they find it and get rid of it."

"Well, I don't want them to kill it."

"I know, silly, but if it's a wild animal, they can take it out to the National Forest and let it loose. The city is no place for a wild animal." Betsy turned and picked up the phone from the receiver.

Amanda stood in shocked silence as she listened to her roommate tell the person on the other end of the phone what had happened.

She knew from Betsy's tone that she and the person on the other end of the phone were questioning her sanity. They lived in a big city, and the closest thing they got to a wild animal was a stray cat or two. They didn't even get raccoons. If there was some huge animal like she thought, then it would make headline news.

Shaking her head in aggravation, Amanda turned toward her room. She suddenly felt silly and didn't want to have to explain what she saw to any more people.

"Amanda? Where are you going? They are on their way and might need to talk to you."

"Tell them it was a dog. Now that I'm thinking about it, it kind of looked like that couple that lives down the road's greyhound. Maybe he just got out."

"Are you sure, Amanda?" Betsy asked, turning and saying something into the phone.

Without saying another word, Amanda shut the door to her room tight and then quickly locked the door. She looked over her room and, seeing the window open and the curtains blowing in the breeze, she ran over to push the window pane down and lock it tight. As she stood there, she looked out into the woods that made up her backyard. There, in the distance, two yellow eyes stared back at her.

Suddenly, more eyes appeared, and it seemed the animals went on forever. She was amazed, since the woods behind her house were very dense and small. The dark night was lit with a full moon. A shiver raced through her as she stood there and stared into the first set of yellow eyes. She quickly shut the curtains and went to sit on her bed. She didn't think she would ever be able to fall asleep knowing what was out there. As she laid her head on the pillow, her mind wondered to large beasts with yellow eyes and sharp fangs. But she was soon fast asleep.

<<◇>>

Amanda awoke with a yawn. It had been almost a month since the incident with what she now called a dog. She had agreed with Betsy that her mind had been playing tricks on her that night. There were often times when she was sure she felt eyes on her, and she would turn in one direction or another, looking. What she was seeking, she didn't know, but somewhere in the back of her mind, she just wanted to know if the eyes she had seen that night had been real or just part of her dreams that evening. She was still so uneasy about it that her walks seemed to get earlier and earlier each evening.

She was just about to walk out the door when her phone started ringing. She quickly grabbed it and pushed the button to answer it.

"Hello."

"Ms. Walker?"

"Yes?"

"Hello, Ms. Walker, my name is Ernest Montgomery. I am calling to tell you that your aunt has passed away."

"My aunt? But I don't have any family. You must have the wrong Ms. Walker."

"No, ma'am. Your father was Joshua Walker, correct? Mother Maureen Walker?"

"Yes."

"Then, I have the right Ms. Walker. It is your father's sister I am referring to. She unexpectedly passed away from a heart attack. I am very sorry for your loss."

"Oh, my gosh! I never knew I even had any family. I am very sad that I didn't get to meet her."

"Yes, ma'am. I'm sure. She was a nice woman. I have also called you to see if you can meet with me. I need to go over her will with you."

"Her will?"

"Yes, ma'am. Your aunt was a wealthy woman."

"Oh? Um, okay. When would you like to meet?"

"The sooner, the better."

"Okay. How about today?"

"That would be great. I am in Slatesville, in the valley."

"Oh. Okay. That is just forty-five minutes from me. I can be there in a couple of hours."

"Sounds good, ma'am. I am at the *Montgomery Law Firm*. I am the only attorney in the town."

"Okay. Thank you, sir. I will see you soon."

"Yes, ma'am. I'll be waiting."

Amanda fell back on the couch, stunned, for what seemed like forever. Everything was pushed to the back of her mind as she thought about what she had just learned. She had a family. Well, she *did* have a family. Now her aunt was gone. Could there be others in her family who she knew nothing about? She didn't know, but she did know one thing. She wasn't going to find out sitting around here, twiddling her thumbs. She needed to get going fast.

Amanda headed for the kitchen. She wasn't surprised to see that no one was there. Of course her roommates weren't home. They were either in class or with their boyfriends.

Smiling, she made a cup of coffee and drank it slowly, thinking about what she might find out. Then, with a deep sigh, she made her way to her car. She looked at the small Honda with pride. It was a pile of junk to some, but it held a special place in her heart. She hadn't been able to get rid of her father's car. Instead, she had sold her own.

She looked down at the small picture he had taped to the dash near the speedometer. She was about six in the picture, and she had been holding her mom's cheeks in her hands as she kissed her.

She remembered the day like it was yesterday. They had just got to a cabin they vacationed in. She had enjoyed herself so much. The little cabin had one bedroom with a queen-sized bed where her parents slept and a set of bunk beds for her. They had stayed up late roasting marshmallows as her father told her scary stories about wolves and vampires. She had ended up in their bed, snuggled between the two of them. They had spent the next day hiking and walking trails and seeing tons of waterfalls and animals.

She had loved it and had never forgotten. It soon became a family tradition to go camping every year. After some of those trips, they didn't return home.

Instead, they moved on to a different location. The constant moving had been hard on her as a kid, but she would have never told her parents that. She had felt like they were hiding something from her. Of course, she had been young back then and had blown it off as childhood curiosity. Now, with this new family member, she wasn't so sure.

Her parents had been very quiet people. They seemed cautious of everything going on around them and were even a little jumpy at times. Maybe there was more going on here than she thought. She needed to find out.

She wiped away a tear and go in the car. The car had a huge dent in one side and was almost fifteen years old, but it got her where she needed to go. She slid the car into drive and smiled to herself.

"Dad would be proud that his car was still running so good, wouldn't he, Trixy?" She and her father had named the car together.

Amanda turned onto the next road and made her way down the narrow two-lane road that led into the mountains. She had never been this way because her parents always went the long way around the mountains. They said they liked to take the scenic route.

She came to a small wooden sign that said *Slatesville—Welcome to your home away from home*. She smiled at the welcoming sign and kept on her way to the town. As she drove, she was amazed at how beautiful everything was. The low-hanging branches of the trees scraped the roof of the car every once in a while.

She was amazed at how many animals she saw. Deer acted as if they weren't afraid of her car. Raccoons were plentiful, and she jumped when a large black snake slithered across the road. There were people all around, and they watched her car curiously as she made her way down the street.

The town reminded her of a long lost western ghost town. It was a little spooky, and she caught herself checking the doors to make sure they were locked. The men nodded at her as she moved forward and many of the people smiled, although they held themselves back a little.

Amanda finally saw the sign that said *Montgomery Law Firm*. She pulled into one of the many vacant parking spots and slowly got out of the car. A handsome man leaned against the building she was about to enter. His brown eyes had flecks of yellow and orange in their deep depths. She smiled slightly, and the man just continued to stare as he looked her over slowly.

"Can I help you, ma'am?"

"I am just here to see Mr. Montgomery."

"Well, you're in the right place, Miss…?"

"Oh, Amanda. Amanda Walker. And you are?"

Something changed in his eyes as he smiled at her and made his way to her side. He held out his hand to her. "Name's Curtis Livingston."

"Oh. Do you live here?"

"Yes. I'm one of the controlling partners here in Slatesville. Well, I have to be going. It was good to meet you."

"You, too, Mr. Livingston."

"Please, call me Curt. Everyone does."

"Only if you call me Amanda."

"That's a deal, sweet lady." She flushed all over when he raised her hand to his lips and gently caressed her knuckles with a brief touch of his mouth. She felt the rise in temperature in her cheeks spread across her upper chest. She stood there and watched as he walked away from her down the street to slip inside a store. She felt foolish and realized that she had been staring. She shook her head, trying to think straight and clear the thoughts that were running through her mind.

Amanda was always aware that she wasn't the Barbie doll type of girl. Although she wasn't fat, she wasn't rail thin, which most men liked, either. Her waist and stomach didn't look like a washboard, although it didn't look like a bunch of bread dough either.

She instantly felt inadequate and quickly turned around to walk to the door of the attorney's office. Knocking, she was surprised when the door instantly opened. The man who opened the door wasn't what she expected. Mr. Montgomery was a short, pudgy man. He didn't wear a business suit, and he didn't seem stuffy at all. He was older and had a short goatee around his mouth. His hair was pulled back into a ponytail at the back of his neck, and he smiled when he saw her.

"You must be Amanda. You look just like your father, except for your eyes. You have your mother's eyes. Let's hope you didn't inherit your father's temper, though," he chuckled.

"You knew my father?"

"Oh, why yes, my dear. We grew up together, Josh and I. Have to say we got into a lot of trouble as kids, and your aunt Mabel was always there to wag her finger and tell on us. You see, there were the three of us; Joshua, Jeremiah, and I. We were called the three musketeers. Mabel wanted to be the fourth, but you know boys. We would never let her, so she always ran and told on us to get back at us for not including her; the little minx." He told the story fondly, and she instantly knew that this man held her family in the highest regard. She also knew he was her ticket to finding out the truth about her family.

"Do I have any more family that I don't know of?" She held her breath, as though she were a child again, asking if Santa Claus was real.

"I am sure you do, my dear. Unfortunately, your aunt was the last of your father's line. She couldn't have any children, and most of the family was killed in a fire in '90. I am sure there is still family on your mother's side, though. However, I must warn you that they are not the kind of people you want to know. Now, if you will come in, I will tell you about everything that now belongs to you."

"What?"

"Oh, my dear, you must know that your father's family had a legacy. You are the only Traverse left to take over the family business."

"What? I don't know what you're talking about."

"They never did tell you who you really are, did they? Oh, you poor child. I am afraid you are going to learn some things about yourself that are going to be hard for you. You must still be a virgin as well."

"I beg your pardon, sir, but I don't see how that's any of your damn business."

"No, my dear, I do not mean to be crude. I was just saying that you have never undergone the Change. It will happen, though. You recently turned twenty-four, and everything changes now."

"What change? What in the hell are you talking about?"

"They hid that from you, too? Oh my gosh. You don't know? Oh, Lord. Okay, first things first. You are now the owner of your family's estate."

"Family estate? So I have a house."

He smiled kindly at her. "Not just a house, my dear. It is what holds the legacy of your family name together. The estate has fifteen bedrooms with their own bathrooms and fireplaces, a kitchen, dining room, parlor, living area, office, library, Carolina room, staff quarters, wrap-around porch with two different sections screened in, pool, tennis courts and 300 acres. It was the pride and joy of your ancestor, Edgar. He was a distant grandfather of yours."

"Oh my gosh."

"Yes, ma'am. How about this? How about I get the keys and directions to the place? You go take a look at it, and then we can talk tomorrow about what you want to do. Stephan has been looking over things, and since your aunt's death, he has given everyone time off until you arrive and decide where to go from there."

Amanda wasn't sure she had the energy to deal with all of this tonight. "Unfortunately, it is very late. Is there somewhere that I can stay for a couple days and then I can go from there and take the day tomorrow to go look at the place?"

"That is perfect. Just give me a second, and I'll find a place for you to stay tonight."

Amanda sat quietly and listened to him talk on his phone. She didn't even hear his words as she thought of what she was going to do.

"I have gotten you a little cabin to rent down the road," he said, drawing her attention back to him. "It is in the woods a little but has electricity and such. On such short notice, I couldn't find anything else. It is only about ten minutes away. The key will be under the mat at the front door. Just go on in and make yourself at home."

"That is perfect. Thank you so much."

"You're welcome, my dear, and we will talk tomorrow. Say ten o'clock tomorrow morning? We will meet here and go to see the house together."

"Perfect. Thank you, Mr. Montgomery."

If you enjoyed this sample then look for **Romeo Alpha: A BBW Paranormal Shifter Romance - Book 1 by Darla Dunbar**.

Other Books by Carla Coxwell

- <u>Fifty Recipes For Disaster New Adult Romance Series </u>(This series precedes "<u>Star Bright New Adult Romance Series</u>")

- Torrid Exposure New Adult Romance Series

- Devil's Advocate BBW MC New Adult Romance Series

- Obsessed Bounty Hunter Romance Series

Get the latest update on new releases from the author at:

https://www.carlacoxwell.com/newsletter

About the Author - Carla Coxwell

Carla has always been a fan of romance novels. To augment what she made waiting on tables to help her way through college, Carla also did some freelance work in the romance genre.

Now she enjoys living vicariously through her characters in her New Adult Romance books.

Connect with Carla Coxwell

I really appreciate you reading my book! Here are my social media coordinates:

Friend me on Facebook:
https://www.facebook.com/CarlaCoxwell/

Follow me on Twitter: https://twitter.com/carlacoxwell

Check me out on Goodreads:
https://www.goodreads.com/author/show/10691544.Carla_Coxwell

Subscribe to my newsletter:
https://www.carlacoxwell.com/newsletter/

Visit my website: https://www.carlacoxwell.com/